BRING BACK YESTERDAY

Jo was shocked to find that Adam Roker now owned the land on which stood the restaurant she had worked to build up — and her home — for he was the man who had walked out on her eight years before, and the father of her child. But, whatever financial power he now had over her, Jo knew that she must never let him know that Jon was his son . . .

BRING BACK YESTERDAY

BY
RACHEL FORD

MILLS & BOON LIMITED
ETON HOUSE   18–24 PARADISE ROAD
RICHMOND   SURREY TW9 ISR

*First published in Great Britain 1987
by Mills & Boon Limited*

© Rachel Ford 1987

*Australian copyright 1987
Philippine copyright 1987
This edition 1987*

ISBN 0 263 75834 6

*Set in Baskerville 10 on 11¼ pt.
01-0887-53446*

*Computer typeset by SB Datagraphics,
Colchester, Essex*

*Printed and bound in Great Britain by
Collins, Glasgow*

CHAPTER ONE

THE doorbell rang loudly, just as Jo spotted the missing toy soldier. Bobbie, no doubt, come to tell her that she had locked up over in the restaurant, and to see how Jon was.

'Come in—he's sound asleep,' she called through the open hall door, but the only reply was another insistent peal on the bell.

For heaven's sake! Jo tossed the soldier into the toy box, flung down the lid and hurried into the dimly lit hall. If Jon woke now, she could forget all ideas of a leisurely bath and an early night—she would be up until midnight. She threw open the door, but the words froze on her lips as she saw not her young assistant but the outline of a man, framed against the darkness. Jo's hand tightened on the door-knob and she made an instinctive movement to draw back. Then, in that same instant, she became very still, her eyes dilating in disbelief. It was Adam.

Adam Roker was the first to recover. He gave a slight laugh and said, 'Well, well . . . I suppose I should say, "Of all the bars in all the world, she has to walk into mine!" But that isn't quite appropriate.'

Then, as she still stared up at him speechless, her eyes enormous with shock, he added impatiently, 'Well, do I get an invite in—or are you going to stand here all night looking at me as though I'm a ghost?'

But you *are* a ghost! she shrieked inwardly. A ghost that I thought I'd exorcised long ago!

'W-what do you want?'

There was a tinge of bitterness in his laugh. 'That's a nice welcome, I must say—after all this time. Actually, I was expecting to see your aunt, Miss Thornton. Is she in?'

Jo's grip tightened even more on the door-knob, clammy against the cold metal, but with a supreme effort she pulled herself together. 'Aunt Joan's dead.' Her voice was strained. 'She died three months ago.'

His expression changed fleetingly. 'Oh, but when they said—I'm sorry.' But she cut him short.

'Why should you be? You always hated her.'

He seemed about to protest, but merely said, 'Look, Jo— can I come in?'

Come in! Horrified, she instinctively went to close the door in his face but he swiftly put up a hand and forced it back.

'Don't worry.' His voice was hard. 'It's purely business.'

Silently, Jo opened the door wider and gestured him in. His bulky frame all at once made the tiny hall seem even smaller but she stalked past him and he followed her into the sitting-room, ducking his head in the low doorway. Her silence masked a multitude of emotions. Intense anger, even rage. *Why* had he come back now, eight years too late? Apprehension. And, above all, a deep thankfulness that Jon was in bed and asleep, the room purged of all evidence of his very existence.

In front of the fire, Adam turned to look at her and, with a huge effort, she gathered to herself some shreds of composure.

'Please sit down,' she said in her coolest voice. 'Can I get you a drink?'

She was pleased that her tone was so detached, so businesslike, that she might have been talking to one of her wholesalers, and he gave her a long look before saying, his voice as cool as hers, 'Thank you, yes—I think I could do with one. A small Scotch would be fine.'

He lounged back on the sofa, with every sign of ease, as

Jo delved into the sideboard for one of a pair of unopened bottles of old malt whisky which a grateful supplier had presented to her at Christmas. As she straightened up, she saw on the sideboard the large, old-fashioned silver frame with two photographs—one of her aunt holding the white bundle that was the week-old Jon, and the other of Jon in his new uniform and satchel almost as big as himself, taken on his first morning at school. In a lightning movement, almost without conscious thought, she scooped up the heavy frame and laid it face down behind the fruit bowl.

She poured a generous whisky, hesitated, then poured a slightly less generous one for herself. When she turned, Adam was looking at her, his dark eyebrows raised, but he only thanked her politely. Total disbelief as to the reality of his presence had been succeeded by a numbed outrage and Jo shivered as she felt a chill settle on her. She turned up the gas fire, sat down in an armchair and took a sip of her drink. For some seconds the only sound in the room was the purring of the gas jets, but she was intensely conscious of his dark eyes regarding her.

After one sip, she set down her glass on the coffee-table and as she did so her arm brushed unsteadily against the jug of yellow daffodils. Their sweet, spicy scent filled the room and she glanced down at the flowers, her lips tightening. Was it only that afternoon that she had seen them in the garden, their cheerful, dancing trumpets braving the chill, buffeting wind and so exactly matching her own sudden, totally unexpected mood of bubbly elation? It's over, she had told herself, it's over. After so many years, I'm beginning again!

Hugging this marvellous new sensation to her, as something very precious, she had brought some of the flowers into the house. But then, just as she was arranging them, the phone had rung.

'Jo? It's Mark here. How are you?'

'Oh, fine, thanks.' But Jo had felt a twinge of unease. Mark Sinclair, her aunt's and now her solicitor never wasted his valuable time on trivial calls—not nowadays, at any rate. 'There's nothing wrong, is there? Don't tell me the estate's doubling the rent for Pear Trees—I don't know that I could manage two pounds per annum!'

But he had not responded to her flippant tone. 'I've just heard that Mr Lydiatt died last week.'

'Oh, no, poor Mr Lydiatt,' Jo had put in softly, but a snort of derision came down the phone.

'Poor Mr Lydiatt my foot! Ninety if he was a day, and at death's door for years! But I'm afraid it could be bad news for you, Jo.'

'Yes, he was always very kind to me. But, as you say, he *was* very old—and of course it does mean that Pear Trees will come to me now.'

There had been a perceptible pause, then, 'How much did Miss Thornton tell you about her affairs?'

'Not a lot, I suppose. She always said I had enough to bother about. But, as you know, she's left everything to me in her will, and that includes Pear Trees.'

'I'm sorry, Jo, but whatever she may have led you to understand, you have no legal claim on the Lydiatt estate.'

'B-but I don't understand,' Jo had stammered.

'Look, you know most of the story, but I'd better go through the whole thing with you. Your aunt worked for thirty years as cook/housekeeper to old man Lydiatt. By all accounts, he became very fond of her—not that that would have done him much good. She was no more the marrying kind than you are.' A hint of reproach had entered his voice. 'Anyway, as you know, when he went off to live in Cannes and the manor was shut up, he leased the old farmhouse and three acres of land to her at a peppercorn rent with the promise, I know, that it would be left to her in his will—or to you, if she died first. Being a wily old devil, he couldn't bring himself to give away a chunk of his estate in his lifetime, I suppose.'

'But surely, that's the way it is.' Mark's sombre tone had been almost frightening and Jo's voice had shaken slightly, the last champagne bubbles of her earlier elation evaporating fast. 'Aunt Joan would never have invested so much money and effort into the property if there hadn't been that understanding.'

'Understanding, maybe, but there's nothing in writing. It should all have been made legal and watertight years ago! I went on and on at your aunt but she always insisted that Mr Lydiatt would have seen to it all and she wasn't going to pester him, look as if she was money-grubbing.'

In spite of her rising anxiety, Jo had half smiled to herself. How like Aunt Joan that was—rigid, scrupulous, a backbone of steel.

'When she died, we dared not wait any longer. We didn't tell you, I'm afraid—I took that responsibility on myself. If everything was all right, it would only have worried you unduly, and besides—I was afraid you'd be just as awkward as she ever was. We contacted Mr Lydiatt's London solicitors but they were very cagey. ". . . assure you we will look into the matter . . . Mr Lydiatt unfortunately too ill to be consulted at present . . ." A polite brush-off, in fact, but we were pressing them and then today came the bombshell. The only will is one dated forty years ago. There's no mention of your aunt, and no codicil relating to Pear Trees or the land.'

'But—there must be some mistake. There *must* be a later will!'

'I don't think so. They'll have checked and double-checked. And,' he had paused, 'I'm afraid it's even worse, Jo. The estate's already up for sale—talk about indecent haste. In fact, it must have been all set up in advance—and a consortium in the City is showing interest.'

Jo had fought down the panic that was threatening to overwhelm her. 'What you're saying is that Pear Trees, the restaurant and garden that Aunt Joan—and I—have spent years creating out of nothing—I've lost it!' Her voice was shaking and she had gone on slowly, as her world crumbled around her. 'There must be something I can do, Mark. Surely, its position on the edge of the estate means that it could be sold off separately. I obviously couldn't buy it outright—not with the overdraft I've got already for the renovation and the new kitchen equipment. But I could pay a fair rent to the new owners—and, the way things are going, I might even be able to put in an offer in a few years.'

'Well, maybe——' Jo had been irritated by Mark's note of professional caution '——but if this syndicate does decide to buy, I'm not sure that you'd want them as your landlords, even if they allowed you to stay. You see, I've heard on the grapevine that they've got plans for the estate.'

'Plans? What sort of plans?'

'Well, I gather that they're hoping to turn it into some sort of gigantic wonderland amusement complex.'

'A what?'

'You know—roller-coasters, wall of death, power-boats on the lake. All good clean fun, no doubt, but hardly the thing to boost Pear Trees' up-market image.' Taking advantage of her stunned silence, he had hurried on. 'Look, Jo—you've got eighteen months before the present lease runs out. As your solicitor, I strongly advise you to cut your losses and put what's left of the lease up for sale now. If we move fast, we could even get a sale before the syndicate's plans are common knowledge.'

'No!' Jo had spoken more violently than she had intended. 'I'm not just walking out. Aunt Joan put so much of herself into Pear Trees—I owe it to her to stay. And besides, it's my home and I love it. I can't—I won't give it up at the first whiff of trouble, not when it's all just beginning to come together. There's that *Oaks to Acorns* slot on TV I told you about—I'm going up to London soon to see the producer. Oh, and next week a journalist from one of the Sunday supplements is coming to interview me— they're doing a new series on good eating in the backwoods. No.' Her mouth had set in a mutinous line. 'Thanks for your advice, Mark, but I'm not throwing all that away.'

'But the wonderland? Surely your image won't stand up to a pool full of sea-lions the other side of the hedge?'

'Oh, with three acres between us it surely wouldn't be that intrusive,' Jo swept on with new-found enthusiasm. 'And anyway, aren't we rather jumping the gun? This syndicate may decide the estate isn't suitable. And they may not get planning permission—I imagine there'll be plenty of opposition locally.'

'Well ... all right. But things are moving fast. I've already had a phone call from a representative of the group, asking—no, telling me that he's coming down to look over the estate—and that includes your patch, I'm afraid. He made that very clear.'

'Oh, don't worry. I'll be able to handle him, even if he does appear in a puff of black smoke!'

'At least promise me you won't do anything to jeopardise your position.' Mark had still sounded worried. 'You can be as difficult and pig-headed as your aunt when you choose to be.'

Jo had laughed wryly. 'Thanks. I take that as a compliment. And don't worry about me misbehaving. I won't throw him down the old well. You never know, I may even invite him in for a civilised drink!'

But as she had put down the phone, the spurt of optimism was already fading. There had been so many unanswered questions. If the syndicate did buy the estate, would they be prepared to let her stay on? Would she want to? Would they grant her a realistic lease? And anyway, she had acknowledged, Mark was right—could the sophisticated ethos of Pear Trees, so carefully nurtured by her aunt, possibly survive a leisure complex as a near neighbour? Aunt Joan—Jo bit her lip. For the first time, her aunt was not here for her to turn to, as she had done at the other times of great crisis in her life; first, when her parents had been killed in a car crash when she was ten and Aunt Joan had whisked her off to the manor to bring her up as her own child, and then, years later, when she had so staunchly stood by her in that hour of even greater need . . .

'This is a very pleasant room, Jo.'

She dragged herself back from the dark chasm of the past to be aware of Adam's voice. As his gaze swept critically over the sitting-room, she was glad, in spite of herself, that there was nothing to be ashamed of. On the contrary, she thought with pride, the soft green velvet suite was comfortable, even luxurious, while the pieces of mellow antique furniture picked up by her aunt over many years, as finances would allow, fitted in perfectly with the oak beams and the hollyhock chintz curtains.

'Yes,' he went on, 'I wasn't quite sure what to expect.' He looked at her quizzically, but when she did not respond, he continued, 'The young lady I met in the restaurant said I'd find Miss Thornton over in Pigsties—why on earth Pigsties?'

Jo forced herself to reply. 'When Aunt Joan took over the farmhouse it had a large stone barn in the yard—a hay-loft up above and a cow byre and pigsty beneath. She had her own flat above the restaurant but decided we—I needed a little place of my own, so she renovated it for me. We're sitting in the cowshed now, and the kitchen was the pigsty. Jon called the house Pigsties and the name's stuck.'

She did not realise what she had said until he queried, 'Jon?'

'Oh—a friend,' she replied—too quickly, but he did not seem to notice so she went on, 'You said you'd come to see my aunt on business?' Her voice was matter-of-fact, but her heart was still beating fast from the slip she had made. But then, before he could answer, the memory of what Mark had said jolted her and she blurted out, 'Oh, good heavens, you're the man from the syndicate!'

He set down his glass. 'Yes, that's right. I'm the man from the syndicate.'

'And I suppose they've sent you down to survey the spoils of war.'

He smiled faintly. 'Well, yes, in a manner of speaking, you could say that.'

'What precisely is this syndicate, anyway?'

He looked at her consideringly for a moment. 'Well, they're headed by Sir Giles Wetherby. I don't know if you've heard of him, but he's pretty big in the City. They started off in oil—that's how I got involved—but now they're branching out into the leisure market—grouse moors, satellite TV—that sort of thing.'

'Oh, so I suppose we can look forward to weekend shooting parties and lines of receiving discs marching across Compton Downs!'

'Something like that, I should think.'

Her sarcasm had merely served to strengthen the steel in his voice, so she changed tack once more. 'Why did you want to see Aunt Joan?'

'To try and sort out this bother over the lease. Look, Jo,' a hint of anger had entered his voice, 'I can see that you'd far rather I were a million miles away, so I'll finish my drink and go. There's no need for you to concern yourself with it all—I'll see your aunt's solicitors in the morning and they'll no doubt be able to fill me in on who's taken over the running of this place.'

'Well, actually, I have.'

'You?'

It gave Jo great satisfaction to see his stunned reaction, but his next words gave her much less pleasure.

'But—you can't possibly——' He broke off when he saw her face, then went on, 'But you're far too young for anything like that!'

'I'm nearly twenty-six, Adam—or had you forgotten? Surely, I'm still eight years younger than you.'

There was an edge in her voice to which he responded in kind. 'Oh, certainly. And that makes me an old man of thirty-four—with a few grey hairs to prove it.' He smoothed back his thick, dark hair which was indeed slightly flecked with grey.

'Oh, no one would guess you're that elderly, I'm sure,' she retorted.

She realised she was being childish but did not seem able to stop herself. She had so often thought about Adam in her dreams—and her nightmares—and here he was, this man who had torn her apart, had wounded her so deeply that she would never again be a whole person. Forcing herself to look, really look at him for the first time she saw, with a surge of annoyance, that he had hardly changed. True, the good-looking young man had vanished, but only to be replaced by a suavely handsome, poised man. He seemed even larger, more intimidating, and the early impression he had given of coiled power which had first drawn to him the shy seventeen-year-old student had been more than fulfilled. Still, she too had changed, she reflected, inside even more than out, and she was now much more his equal, she told herself stoutly.

Aloud, she said, 'I'm afraid I *am* in charge, Adam. You'll have to deal with me—although, of course, there's always Mark.'

'Mark?'

'Yes, Mark Sinclair. My——' for some strange reason, she found herself wanting to say 'fiancé', but added instead, '——my solicitor.'

'Fine. I remember now—I've got his phone number among my papers. I'll give him a ring tomorrow.'

His voice was brisk and he seemed about to dismiss the topic but Jo persisted. 'Why exactly did you come down?'

'Oh, just to see the lie of the land—you know. The purchase of the estate isn't by any means settled, and I thought I'd have a look round. The manor house itself has got a bit run-down, I gather, and the grounds, apparently, are even worse.'

Jo remembered the gardens, the woodlands, the secret pool hidden among the rhododendron walks, a grey stone Neptune presiding over it. The estate had been her playground when she was a lonely little girl, her refuge in all the bad times for so many years. Temper rose in her at his dispassionate tone and she burst out, 'Of course, you people—you only see it as pounds and pence. You can't be expected to see the beauty of it—just whether a Big Wheel will fit on the terrace and whether the lake can be used for water-skiing.'

Adam regarded her coldly. 'Well, I could say that if we go ahead, the estate will give a hell of a lot more pleasure to thousands of people than it ever did to one old man, who sat in the middle of it for years like a spider and no doubt employed armed keepers to ensure that the riff-raff stayed on the other side of the fence.'

'Oh, be careful—your prejudices are showing.'

'My——?Well, OK I've never made any secret of the fact that I came up the hard way, from nothing—at least, that's the way your aunt always saw it. But my prejudices, as you call them, have nothing to do with it. The estate is in a bad way and most of the land isn't particularly good for agricultural purposes. Is the house to be left to fall down or be demolished—or turned into high-quality, high-priced flats for a dozen well-heeled people who fancy a country address like Lydiatt Manor? Surely you haven't turned into such a snob, Jo, even with the superb example of your aunt before you?'

'You leave Aunt Joan out of this.' Jo spoke between her teeth.

'Gladly! I thought I was long ago inured to her hold over you, but obviously I can still feel an odd twinge. Look, it's unfortunate—for both of us—that you're so closely involved, but we've got to be civilised about this.'

Civilised! It was the very word she had used to Mark just a few hours previously, and here she was spitting like a wounded tiger. She drew a breath and went on in a slightly calmer tone, 'And what about this place—Pear Trees? That figures in your syndicate's plans, I take it.'

He was evasive. 'Well—nothing's decided yet, of course. On paper, the restaurant—plus the three acres—are a desirable asset, but well—we'll have to see. Your aunt put a lot of money into it, I believe.'

'Yes,' Jo replied bitterly. 'She never doubted that one day Pear Trees would be hers.'

He shrugged. 'Well, these things happen. Don't count your chickens and all that.' He glanced at his watch. 'Anyway, I must be going, I've got a fair bit of paperwork to do when I get back, and a couple of long-distance calls to make.'

'Where are you staying?'

'Stonegates House Hotel.'

'Oh, you should be quite comfortable there.' Her careful, hostess voice was cool but he sat forward, his dark eyes gazing at her with a sudden, disconcerting intensity, then said, 'And—how are you, Jo?'

'Oh—I'm fine. The—the restaurant's going very well.

We're building up quite a reputation.'

'The place doesn't seem to be exactly jumping tonight,' he observed.

'No, we're closed on Mondays. But tomorrow night we've got an engagement party for the Sanderson girl— they're a big local family. It's quite a feather in our cap.'

'Really?' Jo was gratified that he seemed genuinely impressed. No bad thing, she thought, if the syndicate really were going to be her new landlords. But then his expression changed and he went on, 'No, not the business— I meant you.' He regarded her thoughtfully. 'You've changed a lot, you know.'

There was a note of regret in his voice which stung her. 'What did you expect to find, Adam? This is Pear Trees cottage—not Sleeping Beauty's Castle of Thorns! People grow up, you know. They have to—quite quickly, sometimes. I'm not still the dewy-eyed seventeen-year-old catering student you used to know.'

'I can see that well enough.' His tone was deliberately light. 'But we can all hope. I suppose I've carried an image in my mind for eight years—a golden-haired, sparkling girl in a pink dress—and now I realise that she doesn't exist any more.'

He hesitated, as if waiting for her to speak, but when she did not reply he went on, 'Don't get me wrong—but you *have* changed so.'

'So you said.' She lowered her green eyes so that he would not see the anger flashing in them. She would not allow herself to be wounded by his remarks—he wasn't worth it. 'Now, let me see you out.'

She stood up but he ignored the hint and remained seated. Glancing casually at her hand, he asked, 'You're not married, are you?'

Startled, she met his eyes for a moment. 'No—I'm not married.'

'I just wondered if you'd—well, come through a messy divorce, or something. You used to light up any room you came into, you know. Everyone would turn to look at you.'

Oh, God, she thought, I can't stand much more of this! But she somehow shrugged and said calmly, 'And how about you? Success with all your world-shaking ideas, I hope?'

His eyes glinted, but he merely said, 'Well—some of them. I seem to remember I had quite a few big plans in the old days.' He pulled a wry face. 'I must have been pretty unbearable, I should think.'

She wanted to scream out at him. Why, Adam? Why did you do it? I loved you more than anything in the whole world, and you left me without a word!

Instead, she put down her glass, the whisky hardly touched, and said, 'Yes, you were—unbearable, I mean.'

He laughed unaffectedly. 'That's more like the old Jo-Jo. Truth at all costs.'

Her voice was tight. 'Don't call me Jo-Jo. I've left that silly baby name behind—and anyway, no one ever used it except you.'

He got to his feet and stood very close to her, so that she caught the faint tang of his aftershave. She was uncomfortably aware of his height, and in the small, neat sitting-room he looked out of place somehow, the dark, well-cut suit and white shirt revealing, not masking, his powerful body. Unwillingly, she raised her eyes to his, to find him still watching her. His dark, keenly intelligent eyes had always been able to penetrate her thoughts. She turned her eyes away quickly, but he took her slim hand in his, so that she could not draw away.

'Look, Jo——'

There was a sudden bump, then a wail, from overhead and she snatched her hand away.

'Can you let yourself out, please? I—I must go upstairs

for a moment. Goodnight.'

Abruptly, she left him, still standing in the middle of the room, and ran upstairs two at a time. Jon was in a heap beside his bed, his duvet mounded over him. He was already nearly asleep again and by the time she had soothed him, lifted him, protesting, and tucked him firmly in, he was sound asleep.

Very gently, she disengaged her hand from his. She smoothed her son's soft fair hair and stood looking down at him. The angelic face wore the naked vulnerability which, as always, tore at her heart, making her desperate to protect and cherish him. Was this the child, she asked herself, who a few days previously had got himself involved in yet another scrap at school, and had thrown such a tantrum that she had been sent for? Attention-seeking was the school's diagnosis, deliberately working himself up into a hysterical state, so that she would have to drop everything and go running to him.

With painful self-honesty, Jo acknowledged that they were right. But no matter how often she vowed that she would not let it happen again, as soon as one of Jon's crises blew up out of a clear blue sky, her barely concealed feelings of guilt—that somehow his outbursts were all her fault—splintered her cool veneer once more. Jon had her love—all of it—but too often he didn't have her time and attention. Yet again, she silently vowed that very soon she would detach herself, step back ever so slightly from Pear Trees, and give more time to her son. But really, after the passions and traumas of the year surrounding his birth, it was inevitable, she supposed wryly, that they should have such an emotionally intense relationship. Asleep, he mirrored her so perfectly. Only when he lapsed into one of his rages would his brows come down imperiously and his brown eyes darken stormily. Then, a spasm of angry pain would twist her heart-strings for a few fleeting seconds. She dropped a kiss on his forehead and turned towards the door.

Adam stood in the doorway, watching the scene, his expression inscrutable. Her stomach gave a violent lurch, but she quietly closed the door and descended the narrow staircase to the hall, leaving him to follow. Ignoring what had just happened, she opened the front door. 'Goodnight, Adam. I can tell Mark that you'll be in touch with him, then?'

She spoke softly, her voice empty of emotion. He put his hand against the door and pushed it to, then taking her arm in a firm grip he steered her back into the sitting-room.

'That was a touching little scene.' His voice was cold.

She shrugged. 'I told you to see yourself out. You didn't have to follow me upstairs.'

'Whose is the child? No—I'll phrase that another way. I saw enough by that bedside light to know that he's yours. You said just now that you weren't married.'

'Yes, that's right—I'm not.'

'You're divorced, then?'

'No—I'm not.' Somehow, she managed to control her rising temper. 'I am not married, and I never have been. Does that answer your question? Not that it's any business of yours, anyway.'

She looked him straight in the eye as she spoke, and his tanned face flushed. Keep calm, she told herself, don't lose your head now. In a few days Adam Roker will have gone. Probably he'll never come back—he need never set eyes on Jon again.

He had turned away from her and was looking through the undrawn curtains to the blackness outside. It had begun to rain and the trickling drops of water gleamed through the glass.

Without looking at her, he said, 'How old is your son?'

'Six.' The glib lie came without a moment's thought. He would never find out the truth—Jon was a slim child, small for his age, and even if Adam did see him again, he would never guess. And there was no one to tell him, she thought, with a surge of bitter gladness. She and her aunt had shared the secret. Now it was hers alone.

'Six!' He advanced on her, threateningly, and she flinched from the anger and scorn in his eyes. 'My God, Johanna. You didn't waste much time, did you?'

'Oh!' She gasped as though he had drenched her in icy water. Instinctively, she raised her hand and slapped his face. All the pent-up violence of her tension and anger went into the blow and he rocked back on his heels. Very pale and breathing fast, she faced him across the hearthrug, quite unable to speak.

'I asked for that, I suppose.' His lips twisted in anger and the words seemed to be torn from him, but they gave her the chance to regain her self-control.

'Well,' she said, with seeming indifference, 'what did you expect me to do—go into a convent to mourn my lost love? Girls don't die of broken hearts these days, if they ever did.'

'No—I suppose they don't.' His voice was hard. 'And maybe it wasn't quite such a misfortune my coming here tonight. At least I can see now that I was wrong—wrong about a lot of things, it seems—and certainly about your having changed. You haven't changed at all, really. Underneath, no doubt, you were always the tough, single-minded young woman I've seen tonight—and I was just too besotted to realise it.'

'You—besotted!' Her laugh was bitter. 'When you went off without a word, without a backward glance. I'd hardly call that besotted!'

As a furious retort sprang to his lips, she cut him off.

'No, Adam—no excuses. Not tonight—not ever!' She suddenly felt very weary. 'It's all water under too many bridges, anyway. You were right—I am a different person. It's just a pity for you that the syndicate sent you—you could have preserved your image of me untarnished by reality. As it is—well, it's too late.' She opened the sitting-room door. 'Please go now. I'm very tired. I've got a long day tomorrow and I need a good night's sleep.'

She walked into the hall, giving him no option but to follow her. Then she turned to him, making herself ask the question. 'By the way, are you married, or divorced—or anything?' She kept her voice light, almost mocking.

'No—I've never married.' His eyes were very steady and there was an expression in them which she could not fathom. 'I think maybe the image of that golden girl was too powerful—she somehow got in the way.'

Jo fought down the sudden dagger-like thrust of pain his words evoked and somehow forced a careless laugh. 'Oh, poor Adam. What a sentimental softie you must have become! And for a girl who doesn't exist!'

She opened the front door. Without another word, he walked past her and was swallowed up by the darkness. She closed the door and leaned against it for support, trembling, as she heard him start his car and drive away.

She had done it. She had frozen him off and he would not return. She went back into the sitting-room and sat down, staring at the flickering gas fire. She had also, she thought, had a revenge, of sorts—although he would never know that, of course.

CHAPTER TWO

'WELL, Jo, we've just got to show them how good we are—
make them see that we're too good to lose, that's all.'

Bobbie's eyes were sparkling with the anticipation of the
battle to come. Just how I was feeling yesterday, thought Jo
wryly, but one single sleepless night and Jon at his very
worst all through breakfast and on the way to school had
knocked most of the fight out of her. She looked round at
her full-time staff, assembled before her in the kitchen of
Pear Trees, her gaze moving from Bobbie to Phil, her
young but highly talented chef, then on to Daphne, the
middle-aged widow who worked for her, not at all for the
money but because of an intense need to fill her life. They
were all watching her intently, with silent sympathy, to see
how she would take this latest blow. My team, she thought,
and felt a surge of deep affection for them all.

She gave her assistant a warm smile. 'I'm glad you feel
that way, Bobbie. But maybe you all ought to rethink your
position. We could work like beavers for eighteen months
and I still might not get the offer of a new lease—or I could
be offered one on terms I just couldn't afford. I'm trying not
to be selfish and although I'd be desperately sorry to lose
you, I want you to know——' she stopped suddenly and
cleared her throat '——I just want you to know that if any
of you decide to go, I shan't hold it against you. You've
earned marvellous references and I'm certain you won't
find it hard to get another job.'

'For heaven's sake, Jo, stop babbling and listen.' Bobbie,
normally so easy-going, looked really cross. 'Since you told

me the set-up first thing this morning, we've talked it over
and we are not going, not any of us. Not, not, not.' She went
on fiercely as Jo tried to speak. 'You and your aunt, you
trained us and taught us everything we know. We're
grateful to you and—in case you didn't know it—we're
very fond of you, Johanna Thornton, and we've no
intention whatsoever of leaving you in the lurch, like rats
off a sinking ship—and anyway, this ship's not sinking!'

'Hear, hear,' said Daphne, and Phil added, 'And if you
want us to go, you'll just have to sack the lot of us.'

Jo tightened her lips and looked down at the tiled floor. A
couple of hours ago, she thought, I was feeling how hard-
done-by I was, but I'm not—with a team like this, I must be
one of the luckiest girls around.

She smiled at them, her eyes bright. 'Thanks, everybody—though I wouldn't have expected any less from you.
Now, we'd better get on——'

'Of course, you could always get to work on that man,
Jo—the one from the syndicate,' said Daphne, with a
knowing look.

'Oooh, yes, that's a great idea.' Bobbie rolled her eyes
appreciatively. 'He's *very* dishy, our Mr Roker—very dishy
indeed, folks. You really ought to try your charms on him,
Jo—or if you don't want to, I certainly don't mind having
a——'

'For heaven's sake, Bobbie, are we going to stand here
chattering all morning?' The words were snapped out
before Jo could bite them back, but she controlled herself
and stood up, reaching for her apron, ignoring their
startled expressions. 'Will you help me with the desserts—
finish the lemon syllabubs, then do the chocolate rum
mousses? And Daphne, will you get on with the vegetables,
please? If you need me, I'll be in the back kitchen finishing

off the *croquenbouche*—it's going to be the centre-piece of the dessert trolley.'

She went briskly through to the small kitchen and closed the door firmly so as not to hear the subdued murmur of voices that broke out behind her. She leaned against the door for a few moments to steady the erratic fluttering of her heart, angry—not with Bobbie and Daphne, who could have no idea of what they had said to offend her—but with herself for reacting so foolishly.

Forcing herself to dismiss thoughts of Adam Roker and of everything else from her mind, she set to work with her usual methodical precision, setting out the rows of tiny choux buns. But even they managed to disturb her—she had made them the previous day just before the telephone call from Mark, the call that threatened to shake her painfully reconstructed world about her ears.

Still, she made herself keep working steadily, whipping the thick cream and piping it into the buns, dipping each in the dark, melted chocolate, then boiling up a sugar syrup. Quickly and deftly, she dabbed in each choux bun, gluing it to its neighbour and building them up into an airy pyramid on the pretty pink china pedestal dish. The layers rose higher and higher, until she put the last bun into place at the topmost point.

Jo stepped back and admired it critically. Yes, it was fine. All that was needed were the half-dozen pink rosebuds she had collected, with the rest of the flowers, early that morning from 'The Flower Bowl' in Broadston—and they would have to be tucked into place at the very last moment. She carried the pedestal dish through into the small cool room—once upon a time the farm dairy, where a long line of farmers' wives had made their butter and cream. She placed it on the far corner of the marble slab, out of harm's way, then drew a deep breath and went back into the main kitchen.

Much later, when Jon had eaten his tea and was already bathed and engrossed in television, Mark rang.

'That man—Roker—he came into the office to see me this morning. In fact,' his tone was slightly aggrieved, 'he was on the doorstep when I arrived.'

Jo was instantly wary. 'Oh, yes,' she said, her tone non-committal.

'I gather that you know each other—from way back.'

'Yes, that's right—donkey's years ago, to be exact,' she added lightly.

A silence hung in the wire between them, then Mark said, 'It seems he had rather a surprise when he arrived at Pear Trees last night—meeting you, I mean.'

'Yes, he did rather. In fact, it was quite a surprise for both of us,' and that's the understatement of the year, she thought. She hesitated, then went on, 'It could be rather difficult for him, knowing me. Can't you suggest to him—or the syndicate—that they send down someone else. They must have other employees they could use—accountants, PR men, dogsbodies—someone else.' Anyone else, it doesn't matter who, she felt like adding.

Mark's laugh was rueful. 'That might be rather difficult, Jo. Didn't he tell you who—or rather, what he is?'

Jo felt the ground tremble slightly beneath her feet, like the first distant warning of an earthquake.

'What do you mean—*what* he is?'

'We-e-ll, I'd be wrong to say that Adam Roker *is* the syndicate—there are quite a few other members—but he isn't exactly a dogsbody. He's one of their key decision-makers. I rang a friend of mine in the City this afternoon—his firm have great respect for Roker apparently. For one thing, he's loaded, absolutely loaded. I'm surprised you didn't realise that, Jo—after all, you know him.'

An unbidden picture came into Jo's mind: the brash postgraduate student, so hard up that he sometimes walked miles across London, after insisting on seeing her back to her girls' hostel, to save a bus fare. And when she had scolded him, his telling her that his mother was putting him and his younger sister through university, scrubbing floors at the local hospital in the early morning and cleaning two offices at night—and anyway, a good walk never did anyone any harm. The young Jo had been made uneasy, almost embarrassed, by his revelations. The older, wiser Jo only remembered the pride and love with which the tough, aggressive young man had spoken of his mother. But she forced her mind away from such thoughts and brought them back to the present.

'N-no, I didn't know. Are you quite sure, Mark?'

'*Quite* sure. Roker's a major figure in this consortium— and no one's going to tell him what to do. But, anyway, I shouldn't worry. As you said, the deal may fall through— they're still weighing up the pros and cons apparently— and as your solicitor, I'll do the negotiating. There'll be no need for you to have anything to do with them—and Roker, in particular—if you don't want to. I'll make sure he realises it's all to be done through me, if that's what you want.'

Ah, but what *do* I want? Jo thought, with a bitter smile, as she put down the receiver. What I want is to wake up and find it's all been a horrible nightmare, and Adam Roker has not burst back into my life like some terrifying spectre from the past.

Her mind slipped back only too easily into the deep grooves it had worn for itself through a long sleepless night: would the consortium decide to buy the estate—and, if so, how much would Adam be in evidence? How could she ensure that he didn't see Jon again? What might he do if he ever guessed the truth? And if the unthinkable should happen, could he—gooseflesh prickled her skin—could he take Jon away from her? Of course he can't—stop getting hysterical, she told herself sternly. He deserted you eight years ago and forfeited all claims, legal and moral, to Jon long ago.

Just for a moment she felt again the grey desolation she had endured when, Adam gone, she had faced the future alone—alone, that is, apart from the unfailing, ever-present love and support of Aunt Joan. Tears of gratitude pricked her eyes at the memory of her aunt's selfless devotion—first for her, then for her and Jon.

But then, later, as she lay on her bed after a quick bath, Jo's thoughts went back inexorably to the episode with Adam the previous evening, seen now in the light of Mark's revelations. She could have curled up with embarrassment—not over the things she had said—they were surely deserved and she did not regret them. But, thrown completely off balance by his totally unexpected reappearance, she had attempted to be so coolly condescending with him, not seeing past the picture she had carried of him in her mind for eight years to the man he was in the flesh.

In the end, she gave up the hopeless struggle to relax and started to get ready. But the nagging worry was still there, vibrating through her whole body, like an aching tooth. Keep calm, she told herself. If Mark warns him off, there's a very good chance you won't even see him again. And, believing what he does about you, he surely won't be in any hurry to renew this particular auld acquaintance!

She combed back her newly washed hair, intending to fix it into a huge knot, low in the nape of her neck, but it was even silkier than usual after a shampoo and in the end,

in spite of the best part of a packet of hairpins, she was
forced to twist it into its usual simple pleat. In honour of the
occasion, she put on some moss-green eye shadow, which
deepened the green of her eyes to a dark jade, and filled in
her lips with a soft pink lipstick. No blusher—she would be
flushed enough by the end of the evening. Just a dab of
powder on her nose, a quick spray of the light cologne she
always used, and she turned to her clothes.

She had several neat lightweight navy dresses, which she
usually wore at night in the restaurant, but this evening,
when she held one of them up on the hanger, she felt a
vague dissatisfaction. Next to it in the wardrobe was her
one really good outfit—a two-piece in cream silk jersey,
which Aunt Joan had insisted on giving her for her
birthday a couple of years previously. It was really too
good, of course, but still, the women guests would be dressed
up to the nines and she didn't want to look too dowdy beside
them. She slipped into it, feeling the same thrill she always
experienced as the soft, cool folds slid down against her
warm skin. She put on the exactly matching cream patent
high heels—no doubt she would suffer for that tomorrow
with aching legs, but tonight, no one was going to say that
the proprietor of Pear Trees was a down-at-heel frump!

By the time Mr and Mrs Sanderson and their guests had
begun to arrive, Jo had completely resumed her role as the
successful and confident restaurateur, her private worries
masked by her smooth professional façade. She escorted the
guests upstairs to the small but pleasant low-beamed
reception room, where the two young women from the
village who were brought in to help on such occasions were
waiting with trays of drinks. In keeping with the friendly
house-party atmosphere her aunt had carefully built up, Jo
did not rush back downstairs immediately but stayed

chatting to the host and hostess, together with their daughter and her fiancé—a shy, fair-haired young man who looked totally overwhelmed by his future father-in-law.

But her mind strayed constantly to what was going on below and after laughing politely at yet another of Mr Sanderson's laboured jokes she excused herself and hurried downstairs. Her hand was already on the kitchen swing-door when she saw, in the entrance hall, Adam Roker. She flushed with anger. What on earth was he doing here? She had made it perfectly clear how important this function was to her, yet here he was, no doubt trying to unnerve her for his own sadistic satisfaction. Well, she would just have to get him off the premises in double-quick time!

As she approached him, she took in the fact that he was wearing evening dress, the immaculate white shirt contrasting with his tanned features and with no warning, her heart did several quick somersaults. Slightly breathless, and furious with herself now as well as him, she completely ignored his 'Good evening, Johanna.'

'I'm sorry,' she said, with all the firmness she could muster, 'but the restaurant is closed this evening.'

'Closed?' His dark eyes travelled upwards, towards the sounds of laughter and chinking glasses. 'It doesn't seem very closed to me.'

'You know very well what I mean. We're not open to the general public—we cannot accept any other bookings tonight.'

His eyes narrowed angrily; he seemed to hesitate momentarily, then said, 'But I'm not *making* a booking. I'm here—and I'm hungry—and I want a meal.'

Jo clenched her fingers painfully into her palms to control her exasperation. How dared he? How dared he come sauntering in, as though he owned the place already, and then deliberately provoke this ridiculous scene? 'I've told you, this is a private function.'

'Ah, yes! The engagement party.' There was a malicious gleam in his eye. 'Well, far be it from me to spoil the young people's pleasure, but if I could have a table——' his gaze strayed towards the far corner of the room '——over there, for instance, I assure you I shall be perfectly inconspicuous.'

Adam Roker perfectly inconspicuous! Jo threw restraint to the winds. 'Oh, yes—an ideal spot for you to keep tabs on what's going on! And that's why you're here, isn't it—to see just how well—or, preferably, how appallingly—we perform, then you can report back on us to your precious syndicate. Well, if you want to snoop, you can just make a reservation first! Goodnight.'

She moved away a fraction too late, and Adam's hand was encircling her wrist in a band of steel.

'But that would ruin the whole object of the exercise, wouldn't it! No, tonight will do me just fine,' he said lazily. 'And don't tell me you can't cope with one extra guest. Efficient businesswoman that you undoubtedly are——' the sarcasm in his voice made her flinch '——surely you've made provision——'

'Ah, there you are, Adam. I was beginning to think you wouldn't make it.'

At Mr Sanderson's avuncular boom, Jo snatched her arm away and swung round. Open-mouthed, she heard, 'Miss Thornton, this is the extra guest my wife rang you about. May I introduce Adam Roker.'

Jo stared up into Adam's eyes, now totally bland and guileless, as he said, 'We have—introduced ourselves.'

'B-but,' Jo stammered, trying to gather together what remained of her thinking processes, 'did you say *guest?*'

The older man's brow furrowed. 'What? Didn't Jean contact you? Oh, dear, it must have slipped her mind—

she's been in a state all day over this party. I really do apologise, Miss Thornton. Adam here just happened to call at my office this morning, mentioned that he was at a loose end tonight, so of course I insisted on his coming along.'

But Jo hardly heard him. Adam had 'just happened' to call on Mr Sanderson! After what she had told him last night, he had deliberately wangled an invitation. And not only that—he had made a complete fool of her! Anger and mortification struggled inside her as she was forced to admit that through her own misplaced aggression she had set a trap for herself, which Adam had been only too happy to spring.

'But I'm sure you'll cope, my dear.' Mr Sanderson's voice was still washing over her. 'Jean would never forgive me if we sent this rogue away—she always says that we owe our villa in Portugal to him!'

Once more, Jo's professionalism came to her rescue. 'Of course we'll cope, Mr Sanderson. Please don't worry—and don't upset your wife. There's no need to mention it. I'll just arrange for an extra setting to be laid.' She gave him a dazzling smile which somehow contrived to exclude completely the man beside him.

'Good, good.' Sanderson put his arm on Adam's shoulder. 'Come on, my boy—let's get you a drink.'

They moved off towards the staircase, Adam's face quite inscrutable after one swift glance of triumph in Jo's direction. As they went, she heard Sanderson's voice, a quarter of a decibel lower, saying confidingly, 'Yes, pity she couldn't be marrying you—this young whipper-snapper . . .' Jo went into the kitchen.

Despite—or perhaps because of—her simmering anger, the evening was a great success, the waves of adrenalin keeping Jo working at peak form. She herself had not left the kitchen, dispatching Bobbie to circulate among the guests and report back to her their appreciative comments. But now that they had reached the petits fours and coffee and liqueurs stage the euphoria faded, to be replaced by total exhaustion. She leaned against the preparation table, longing for the moment when she could kick off her shoes and crawl up to bed.

'Jo—they want you to come in.' Bobbie was standing beside her.

'Go in? No—I'm staying here!' Jo's voice was sharp with alarm.

'Of course you're not. The Sandersons want to thank you personally.'

Reluctantly, Jo stood up. Yes, of course she would go— she was a grown woman, not a silly young girl. Instinctively, however, she tried to smooth back the strands of hair which had escaped from her restraining white cap and wiped her hot face on a clean tea-towel. Bobbie watched with growing impatience and when Jo started to unbutton her white jacket she burst out, 'For goodness sake, Jo, why don't you go and have a shower and put on a new outfit while you're at it!'

She almost dragged her boss to the doorway and pushed her through it. Pinning a smile in place, Jo walked the endless carpet, through a haze of blue smoke, across to the main table, where Mr Sanderson beamed up at her, his rosy face now a deep puce.

'A splendid meal, Miss Thornton—and we've all enjoyed a lovely evening.'

Jo, looking round at the smiling faces, could see that they clearly had, but as she glanced round the room her eyes carefully avoided one table.

'Yes, indeed,' Mrs Sanderson added. 'You've given Philippa an evening she'll remember always with pleasure.'

Jo smiled at her. 'Thank you, Mrs Sanderson. It was *our* pleasure.'

Aunt Joan had always insisted on seeing her guests off, as a final friendly attention, and although Jo wanted nothing so much as to seek sanctuary once more behind the doors of the kitchen, her rigid self-discipline carried her on. She stood in the entrance, shivering slightly in the cold night air, as Mr and Mrs Sanderson, she firmly clutching her husband's car keys, finally walked off towards the car park, from where came the sounds of cheerful voices and shouted goodnights from other guests.

The long evening was over—everything had gone marvellously—and even though she was still smarting from her encounter with Adam, she was at least deeply relieved that he had had the grace to slip away quietly, rather than meet her face to face again.

'Congratulations, Jo. If I might say so, that was a superbly professional display you put on tonight.'

She steeled herself to turn very slowly and meet his sardonic gaze. He was standing just behind her and after the first shock of hearing his voice she found she was able to meet his sombre, unsmiling eyes. She looked at him, taking in again the immaculately cut suit, white evening shirt— everything quietly, unostentatiously expensive—above all, his air of relaxed, confident authority. How could she, accustomed almost daily to seeing well-heeled top-ranking businessmen in the restaurant—how could she have failed to recognise another of the breed? Yet, and she silently acknowledged this to herself, there was something more to Adam Roker. In most cases, fine feathers made fine peacocks, but take away his London suit and shirt, his gold watch and heavy gold signet ring, and she knew he would still look every inch what he was—poised, polished, self-assured. A man to be trusted, but also to be feared. She was also sufficiently objective to be able to see very clearly that this new, mature Adam was even more handsome than the brash young man of eight years ago. It was no doubt just as well that she was now totally immune to his very obvious physical attraction!

He went on. 'Yes—I really must congratulate you.' He smiled faintly. 'No wonder you reacted so badly last night when I asked who was running the place now. I can see it's in very capable hands—your aunt would have been very proud of you tonight.'

Then, as she looked at him doubtfully, he added, 'No, I mean it—she would.' He paused then went on pensively, almost as though thinking aloud, 'You really have changed so much, Jo.'

There was the same tinge of regret in his voice and again it stung her. 'You haven't exactly stayed the same,' she retorted. 'Although I seem to remember that you were always ever so slightly confident and self-assured. But you weren't exactly the well-heeled businessman then.'

He shrugged deprecatingly. 'Well, that was luck to a certain extent—being in the right place at the right time. And choosing my friends carefully—or most of them, at any rate.'

The deep bitterness in his voice shook her, but when she glanced quickly at him the shuttered look was back in his eyes. They had to move off this dangerous ground!

'I'm so glad you enjoyed the meal,' she said reluctantly.

But he did not reply. Instead, his eyes met hers fleetingly and she rapidly withdrew hers. He moved towards her and she stepped back sharply.

'Don't——'

'Don't what? I haven't laid a finger on you.' He raised one sardonic eyebrow.

'You know what I mean—and you'd better be careful how you drive,' she added accusingly. 'You've been drinking.'

He shook his head. 'Not me, Jo—at least, only enough to mellow me slightly. You know I don't drink—or very little.'

His dark eyes seemed to bore into her and she thought suddenly, with something akin to panic, that she preferred the other Adam, insolent, domineering—this Adam was somehow even more insidious, more dangerous. What *was* he trying to do now—remind her of old times, old pleasures—and pains—force her to remember that once upon a time she had known all sorts of things—intimate, tender things—about him? If that was his aim, then he mustn't succeed.

'No, I don't know—how should I?' she said woodenly. 'And now you'll really have to excuse me. I'm needed in the kitchen.'

The front door had swung to and she opened it wide. 'Goodnight, Adam.' Her voice was cool and level and he flushed angrily.

'Of course. Don't let me detain you.'

He swung on his heel and strode off into the darkness.

CHAPTER THREE

'RIGHT, Miss Thornton, I think that's all I need. We should be able to make a really good feature on you and Pear Trees.' The journalist slipped her notebook and pencil into her big leather bag. 'Sorry we can't stay for lunch—from what I've seen it would be a pleasure—but we've got another assignment this afternoon. Thanks, anyway.'

She glanced at her watch and stood up. 'Dave should have set up his shots by now. I'd like some of you and your chef in the kitchen—wooden spoon in hand, that sort of thing. Then some outside—perhaps chef holding a serving dish with one of his specialities. I expect he's got something we could use—if not, we can mug up something.'

Jo, remembering the fridge and marble slab overflowing with suitably photogenic dishes, repressed a smile. 'Oh, I think Phil's prepared one or two items,' she said.

'And then we ought to get a shot or two of the garden. Your aunt making it more or less single-handedly from a rough field—that's a different angle to interest our readers. And I like your plans for extending its use—summer lunches on the terrace, and so on.'

'Mmm, yes, it should be an added attraction,' agreed Jo in a non-committal tone. She had decided to keep quiet about the proposed sale of the estate and its possible repercussions.

'Great!' The young woman looked out of the sitting-room window, across the wooded meadows and farmland behind Pear Trees. 'I quite envy you, you know. What are

37

you—twenty-five? And you've got all this going for you.'
She picked up her bag, missing Jo's look of wry amusement.
'Ah, well, let's get on. We'll start in the kitchen, if you like,
then move outside.'

Jo watched as Phil, resplendent in his chef's whites, posed
self-consciously by the front entrance. Her gaze travelled
past the photographer towards the long, low building of
creamy-grey stone. Home! A fierce, almost primitive surge
of possessive love seized her and she felt a burning anger at
the injustice of it all. Was Fate about to deal her yet another
cruel card? Unconsciously, her lips tightened. The only
things she cared about lay under those soft grey tiles, those
dormered eaves. She would never give them up!

She was glad that the weather was fine. Like all gardens,
hers looked its best under a blue sky and she could see that it
was having its usual impact on first-timers. Aunt Joan had
indeed created a garden from a wilderness and the effect
was simple yet stunning. But right from the beginning it
had been designed so that it almost looked after itself—her
aunt had known that she would never have the time herself,
or the money, to employ an army of gardeners.

There were no intricate flower-beds and long borders,
needing endless attention. Instead, the garden was divided
by high, unclipped hedges of beech and holly into long
winding walks, and round every corner there were hidden,
private nooks—a soggy marsh had been made into a bog
garden, alight at the moment with yellow candelabra
primulas and early cowslips, and there were old green
garden-seats dotted about in arbours overhung by huge
shrub roses and honeysuckle, so that on summer evenings
the perfume made the senses reel. At every time of year
there were beautiful things, carefully planted to look
natural—today, as they walked along, the hedge bottoms

were lit up by wood anemones and primroses, and clumps of paper-white narcissi.

The photographer was packing up his equipment when Jo, glancing past him down one of the long walks which ran obliquely from the house to the stream, saw, with almost total disbelief, the unmistakable figure of Adam. She stuffed her hands into her pockets and bunched her fists until her nails bit into her palms, in an effort to keep her self-control. For a moment, she thought of pointing him out to the journalist and maybe enlisting her sympathy, but thought, no. Publicity, at this stage, might do her more harm than good and, in any case, this was one battle she had to fight herself.

Instead, chatting casually, she steered them back down the walk towards the car park. She kept her smile tacked carefully into place until their car was well out of sight, then it abruptly faded. She strode back towards the garden, her high heels making an angry clip-clop on the gravel. She saw nothing of the garden now, conscious only of a steadily burning sense of outrage inside her. This place was not just trees, plants, it was her beloved refuge, her retreat and no one—least of all Adam—had any right to force their way into it. She felt physically sick, as though she herself had been invaded. The memory of their last encounter—his gloating triumph at her discomfiture—still rankled, but this time surely she was on firmer ground. He was on her territory, and could only have invited himself.

She found him on the far bank of the stream and he stood, hands in pockets, watching as she approached. Her quick eye took in his appearance—beige cord pants, a casual-cut brown leather jacket and cream roll-neck sweater. Huh, quite the country gentleman now, she thought with a spurt of temper. But of course, she admitted sourly, as usual he looked just right and completely at his ease, his glance lazy, ever so slightly mocking. Too late, she realised, as her heels sank in the boggy ground, that she should have changed her shoes.

'I suppose you realise you're trespassing?' She shouldn't have hurried so much, either—her voice, even to her own ears, was breathless.

From his vantage point on higher ground. Adam gazed down at her with languid amusement. 'Oh, for God's sake, Jo, we're not going all through that rigmarole again, are we? I hope you're not going to try and run me off your land again—I'd have thought you'd learned that particular lesson!'

She forced down the retort which sprang to her lips. Softly, softly! If she wasn't careful, Adam's wily brain would somehow contrive to wrong-foot her again, even when he was so palpably in the wrong. The threat of his doing just that was clearly there under the silken tone.

'I was just having a casual look round—no damage done. Well, the odd blade of grass, perhaps!'

'I'm surprised you didn't bring your tape measure!' she snapped. 'And if you—and the rest of your syndicate, for that matter—wish to look over *my* grounds, I'd be grateful if you would make an appointment—which I believe is the proper thing to do.' Her voice crackled with ice. 'And preferably through Mark.'

'Mark? Oh, yes—the solicitor.' Jo flushed with anger—for Mark as well as herself—at his lightly contemptuous tone. 'So he's your Gorgon, is he? Yes, all right, I'll tell them. I imagine they'll be down within the next week or so. Giles was here a couple of days ago to look the place over.'

'Oh, really?'

'Yes, he's got some—interesting ideas for the estate.'

'Isn't he rather jumping the gun? Wouldn't it be wiser to decide whether you're definitely buying before he starts indulging in any fancy ideas?'

'Oh, didn't I tell you? So sorry.' The mockery was back in his voice, the glint of malice in his eyes.

'Tell me what?' she demanded.

Instead of answering her, Adam measured the width of the stream with his eye and leapt across, his long legs easily clearing the narrow ribbon of water to land very near her. Startled, Jo wrenched her heels out of the soggy turf and moved back a few paces.

'Tell me what?' she repeated, a slight tremor in her voice.

'Why—that we've just about decided to buy.'

'You mean *you've* decided!' she burst out, the hostility naked in her tone now.

'Well, yes, I've recommended it—and Giles agrees with me. The whole place is very run-down, of course, but taking a ten to fifteen-year view it should be a sound investment.'

'You said he—your partner—had some interesting ideas.'

'Oh, you know,' he shrugged dismissively. 'Mississippi steam boats on the lake, overhead railway, corkscrew ride down by the woods, fast food and burger grill in the manor. Oh, don't worry—no competition there for you to bother about,' he laughed mirthlessly. 'Yes, I really think this is going to be his baby—he's even got some idea in his head about a chamber of horrors waxworks in the basement!'

Jo steeled herself. What was it Shakespeare said—*to know by the worst means the worst*?

'And—and Pear Trees. Where does that figure in your schemes?' In spite of herself, her voice shook.

'I'm recommending that you be allowed to stay on—at a

market rent, of course.'

'Well, thank you. I'm *so* grateful.'

'Of course,' he went on, as if she hadn't spoken, 'on present form, Giles may well see all this,' he took in the garden with a sweeping gesture, 'as a total waste of useful resources. It would make a crazy golf course, perhaps, or a pets' corner.'

Jo closed her eyes momentarily. Perhaps, she thought, when she opened them again Adam would have vanished, together with the dreadful grinning apparition of Sir Giles. But when she did open them, Adam's eyes were fixed on her face, his own quite deadpan apart from a slight twitch at one corner of his mouth, and suddenly she thought incredulously, he's enjoying this, really loving every minute of it! Perhaps he even hoped she would burst into tears, grovel at his feet for mercy! But he should know that she never cried.

Adam glanced at his watch. 'Well, if there's no more information I can give you—I'm meeting our architect at the manor in ten minutes.'

'You don't waste much time, do you?' Jo's tone was bitter. 'What's he doing—measuring for the burger grill?'

'No, I want him to take a look at my flat.'

'Your f-flat?' she gaped at him.

'Dear me—I didn't tell you. How remiss of me. Yes, I've decided to have a toehold down here—nothing spectacular, but I'll be able to keep an eye on things and, anyway, it'll get me out of London—a spot of rural tranquillity in between overseas trips. I sometimes think I'm getting too old for this if-it's-Thursday-it-must-be-Tokyo lark.'

Jo said nothing. She turned away, knowing that she could not hide the consternation she was feeling. Just a few days ago, she had persuaded herself that with luck she would never see Adam again and that there would be no danger of his ever encountering Jon. And now here he was, about to move in as her neighbour and, unless a miracle occurred, become an almost permanent fixture! Desperately, she shook herself free of the cold panic that trickled inside her. Adam simply must not be allowed to guess the effect his words had had on her.

'Yes,' he was speaking reflectively, 'I suppose I could bring him across to Pear Trees for lunch. Do you keep a food-taster?'

'A food-taster?' Jo's mind struggled to keep up with his train of thought.

'You know—one of those medieval life-preservers, to sample our food. No, on second thoughts it'd better be a pub snack. Delectable though a meal at Pear Trees would undoubtedly be, I simply couldn't trust you not to sprinkle strychnine on my lobster!'

Jo stared woodenly at him. 'I'll warn Mark that your colleagues will be in touch, then.'

Adam gave a furious exclamation and lifted his hands as though he would seize her by the shoulders and shake her, but then his arms dropped back by his side.

'What a buttoned-up, tight-lipped little miss you've become! My God, Jo—that precious aunt of yours did a better job on you than ever she could have intended!'

Shocked, she stared up at him. 'What?'

'Well, look around you.' He spread his arms. 'Spring's here . . . lark's on the wing . . . all's right with the world . . . only Johanna Thornton's walking around with a face like January!'

Jo forced herself to remain impassive at this savage parting thrust. How cruel, how unfair—coming from him, of all people. But how like him. She watched as he leaped the stream once more, forced his way through the thick rhododendron hedge and so out of sight.

Bobbie and Phil stared at her curiously when she came back into the kitchen but she took the proffered cup of coffee in silence, quite unable to speak.

When Jo collected her son from school that afternoon he was in one of his sunny moods and chattered excitedly all the way home on the back seat of the car. She had to do no more than listen and put in the occasional enthusiastic comment. When they got out of the car Jon hugged her, in one of his rare displays of affection. Jo put her arms round him and held him tightly to her, feeling the fierce love and protectiveness he always aroused in her but which she tried not to show too often. He looked up at her, his small face too pale, too thin, she thought, but alight with eager intelligence—and, at present, good humour. They walked together across the courtyard to the front door of Pigsties.

'Can we have one of *our* evenings tonight, Mummy?'

Because of the calls on Jo's time, their evenings were not often completely undisturbed and the little boy resented this.

'Well, no, darling. I'm afraid I shall have to go over to the restaurant later. You know it's Bobbie's night off.'

Jon scowled. 'Why can't *you* have a night off? I want you to have a night off—you never do.'

'Now that's not true, love. I do sometimes. Besides, it's different for me, you know that.'

'Don't see why.'

Jo decided on diversionary tactics. 'I tell you what—we'll have a nice cosy tea by the fire, watching television, and we'll just have time for a game of Snap before I have to change.'

'Don't like Snap.'

'And you can choose what we have for tea—whatever you want. There's some lovely chicken casserole left over.'

'No—fish fingers and beans and chips—and a chocolate mousse.'

Jo laughed. 'All right—fish fingers and chips it is. Now you wash your hands and go and play in the living-room, while I get it.'

As she was in the kitchen cutting up chips, the doorbell rang. She was still drying her hands when she opened the door—to be met by Adam. Her first reaction was one of angry stupefaction. What on earth did he want now? Couldn't he see that all she wanted was for him to leave her alone? But this was followed by a spurt of plain terror, so that she would have slammed the door in his face, had he not put his hand firmly against the panel. Ignoring her hostile expression, he held out a huge sheaf of white and blue iris and pink tulips.

'Peace offering.'

Jo, still raw from his cruel words earlier, hardly glanced at the gorgeous bouquet. 'You needn't have bothered. I don't need your flowers.' She kept her voice almost to a whisper, praying that the living-room door was firmly closed.

'Do take them. I know I did get rather carried away this morning, although you really are enough to try the patience of a saint.'

'Who is it, Mummy?'

To her horror, Jon was beside her, before she had even heard his footsteps. But even at this late stage, she fought against fate.

'Jon, go into the kitchen, there's a good boy, and see—see whether I left the chip-pan on.'

But he pushed past her and the two of them, father and son, stared at each other. A historic moment, Jo thought wildly—what a pity I haven't got the camera! But the hysterical laugh that welled up in her died away, as the full horror of the situation hit her.

'Jon—please do as I asked,' she said, but the boy ignored her, looking hopefully up at Adam.

'Can you mend an inter-galactic space module? Mine's broken.'

Adam grinned down at him. 'Can I mend . . .? I've mended more inter-galactic space modules in my time than you've had hot dinners, I can tell you.'

Jo scowled at him over her son's head. 'Jon, Mr Roker is very busy—he has lots to do. And besides, you have to have your tea,' she added despairingly. After all, short of snatching a struggling Jon up in her arms and kicking the door to in his father's face, there was not much she could do.

Jon seized Adam's willing hand and pulled him in over the doorstep. 'Come on,' he said imperiously, dragging him across the hall and into the sitting-room. As he followed, Adam thrust the flowers into her hands, then looked back over his shoulder with a deprecating shrug. But Jo was not fooled for an instant. She knew suddenly that he had engineered the whole thing—if he really did want to apologise for his behaviour, he could have phoned or come to Pear Trees in the evening. But no, he had deliberately chosen to come to Pigsties. Then a further thought struck her—he must have known that Jon would be with her at this time. Jon! Was he the real reason that he had come? She went through into the kitchen, slammed the door as loudly as she dared and hurled the flowers into the sink. She sat down at the table and beat her fists on it, as the anger and panic welled up in her again.

At last, she calmed down and tried to think rationally. There was no reason to fear that Adam did suspect the truth—his reaction the previous night when she had lied to him over Jon's age showed that he had believed her. Why should he be suspicious now? No—she must play this particular poker game very coolly, very carefully, and she would win. Adam must not think for a moment she had anything to hide and he would then soon lose interest in her and her child.

When she opened the sitting-room door, the two of them were squatting on the rug, side by side. Jon raised a smiling face and held up a toy rocket. 'Mummy, he's mended it—Adam's mended it.'

'I hope you've said thank you to *Mr Roker*, Jon.' Her tone was sharper than she had intended and he hung his head.

'Sorry, Mr Roker—and thank you very much.'

'That's all right, Jon. Glad I could help—oh, and Adam's fine by me.'

The two of them exchanged a smiling look—a look which Jo recognised, of masculine rapport, from which she as a mere woman was definitely excluded. Jon never looked at anyone like that except, very rarely, when he was with Phil. She almost winced at the stab of jealousy it aroused in her. Jon was hers and she would not—could not—share him with anyone—least of all with the man who was his father.

'I've asked Adam if he'd like to stay to tea.' Jon's voice was proprietorial. 'He loves fish fingers.'

'Oh, does he?' replied Jo tartly. Then she saw the puzzlement clouding Jon's eyes and her heart smote her—she must not use Jon as a weapon in this private war. Firmly pushing aside her own feelings, she smiled down at him.

'I dare say we can find him some then, love.'

They ate round the fire, trays balanced on their laps, the relative silence of the two adults masked by Jon's happy chatter. The cosy warmth of the gas fire, the soft glow from the wall lights, toys scattered on the floor—any outsider looking in, thought Jo, would assume that this was a happy family scene, whereas in reality . . . Her lips tightened in pain and she glanced at Adam, to find his eyes fixed on hers, as though he had been reading her thoughts.

He put down his knife and fork. 'Those were the best fish fingers I've ever eaten, Jon,' he pronounced.

'Oh, Mummy's a wonderful cook—everybody says so.'

Jon smiled proudly at his mother and then, almost as if he had sensed the disturbing undercurrent of emotions, he ran across and gave her a hug and a kiss.

'I'll get the chocolate mousses, Mummy.'

When he was safely out of the room, Adam said, 'He's a nice kid, Johanna. You've made a good job of him, single-handed.'

Jo chose to ignore his final words. 'Thank you—although I must admit he's on his best behaviour tonight. He has his off days.'

'Don't we all? But I like him—he's great.'

'He likes you as well, I can see that.' Jo could have bitten her tongue with vexation, admitting it, but it was true— Jon, normally so wary, so withdrawn with strangers, had opened out to Adam on sight.

Clearly choosing his words with great care, Adam asked, 'Does he have any contact with——?'

But she broke in, 'I know what you're going to say, and don't. My private life is nothing, absolutely nothing, to do with you—and neither is Jon's. Please, Adam, leave us alone.'

She jumped to her feet and began collecting the plates

together, as Jon came back, proudly carrying the puddings.

Afterwards, with great reluctance, Jo left them together and went upstairs to change and shower for her evening's work. She put on one of her neat navy wool dresses and sat down at her dressing-table; she took out the pins in her hair and shook it so that it tumbled on to her shoulders. She knew she was already late but nevertheless she sat for a few minutes, studying herself, as though meeting a stranger for the very first time. Her fair hair, as always at the end of a long, English winter, was drab and sun-starved—it could do with some highlights, she supposed, to frame her face more flatteringly. Her complexion, as usual, was pale, lacking make-up, although there was a slight rose flush over her cheekbones this evening. Her eyes, green and enormous, were, she acknowledged, her best feature, but these days they seemed always to look shadowed and anxious. She burrowed in her dressing-table drawer and found a bag stuffed with odds and ends of make up she had not bothered to use for a long time. She found some brown mascara and hesitantly started to apply it. It was quite amazing the difference it made, she thought—it emphasised her eyes, making them seem even larger. Perhaps she would try her hair not in the usual knot, but in a swinging pony tail high on her head.

She stopped and stared hard at herself. What are you doing? she thought. You're mad, quite mad. Adam Roker crashes back into your life and you start behaving like a ridiculous little fool! And not only that, she told herself contemptuously, while you're tarting yourself up to the nines up here, spare a thought for what's going on down below.

She scrubbed at the mascara until her lids smarted, then put on her usual flick of pink lipstick and combed her hair back into its customary smooth knot. 'That's more like it, my girl', she said aloud, and nodded approvingly at her unsmiling reflection.

'I'm afraid Mr Roker will have to be going now, darling,' she said firmly, as the two looked up from their game.

'Oh, Mummy, no—we've only just started.'

'But you told me you don't like Snap,' Jo pointed out. 'And, anyway, I have to go now—I'm late already—so up you get.'

'No. Adam's staying—I want him to.'

'Jonathan—do as you're told!'

'No, I won't! I want Adam to stay and keep me company.'

Impotent fury was rising once more in Jo but she managed somehow to control it. The last thing she wanted now was one of Jon's tantrums although, she reflected sardonically, it might alter Adam's opinion of their son, which would be to the good, at least. She looked down at Jon, scowling darkly up at her from the hearthrug and thought, surely he must see the resemblance. But at that moment, she was almost past caring.

'Look, Jo——' Adam began, but she said, between her teeth,

'Will you please *go*, Adam. He'll be all right.'

As Adam hesitated, Jon played his last card. He began to cry, with loud pathetic sobs. 'Adam said he'll help me with my maths. I told him I got them all wrong today and Miss Smith said I didn't listen, and now I shall have to stay in at playtime . . .' His voice disintegrated into loud wails.

Jo felt as if she were wading through a treacle sea, and sinking at every step. She knew she was being manipulated, but short of having a full-scale scene she could not win.

Jon, sensing possible victory, snuffled, 'Besides, you know I get lonely at night.'

'Now that's nonsense, Jon. I'm only next door—and you've got the internal telephone to Pear Trees. Now you go and have your bath—you can read in bed, and then I'll pop back to settle you down.'

'No—don't want Adam to go away.'

He sat himself down firmly on the rug, as though glueing himself to the pattern.

'You go on, Jo,' said Adam. 'I can see to him, really. I'd be glad to help——'

'But I don't want your help,' Jo snapped bitterly.

Suddenly the frustrated anger that had been simmering since the episode in the garden that morning, coupled with the resentment towards Adam and the shame that he should have witnessed the scene with Jon, seen her so helpless against her son, finally boiled over. Grabbing hold of Jon, she hauled him to his feet and smacked him very hard across his bottom.

She had never laid a finger in anger on him before and almost as the blow was struck she dropped her hand, and they stared at each other in shocked disbelief. Jon's eyes filled with tears, as she knelt beside him.

'Oh, Jon,' she whispered, 'I—I'm sorry.'

Adam's voice cut in. 'Don't apologise, Jo. He asked for it—I felt like whopping him myself.'

His tone was brisk and Jo was amazed to see that, far from resenting it, Jon laughed at him shamefacedly.

Adam went on, 'I really don't want to interfere, Jo, but I had just promised to help him with his maths.'

She opened her mouth to protest, but he went on quickly, 'I've got nothing on tonight—just a boring evening on my own at Stonegates House doing paper work—so you'll be doing me a favour. We'll do the maths, then I'll get him bathed and into bed—read him a story. OK?'

Jo's shoulders drooped from sheer weariness. Why fight any more? She was well and truly beaten. She dropped a light kiss on Jon's head. 'Bye, Jon—see you in the morning.'

She couldn't trust herself to speak to Adam so she just nodded to him and left them to it.

When she returned just before midnight, the hall light had been left on for her. The sitting-room was tidy, while in the kitchen the washing-up had been done and her blue china mug and the tin of drinking chocolate had been put by the stove. She made her drink and carried it upstairs with her. At Jon's door, she stopped and looked in. He was curled up, sound asleep, his teddies standing on their heads in a row against the wall. Jo got into bed and drank her hot chocolate, staring into the darkness beyond the small circle of light around her bedside lamp.

CHAPTER FOUR

Jo dragged up the bonnet and peered into the innards of the car with a feeling of acute hopelessness. The top of the engine was very dirty, so she wiped it carefully with a tissue, then pushed the leads firmly on to the plugs. But the car remained obstinately lifeless. Surely, she thought, there was nothing in this whole world more aggravating than a car which wouldn't go—or rather, which had got her two miles out of Compton Lydiatt, before lurching to a halt and dying on her.

She leaned against the side of the car, chewing her underlip as she thought frantically. She could walk back to the village and phone the nearest garage. She glanced at her watch—seven-fifteen, they wouldn't even be open yet. She could get Bobbie to run her down into Bristol to catch a London train—but she would never make it in time. A taxi? She shuddered at the cost, even supposing she could persuade the single taxi owner in Broadston to venture so far off his familiar patch.

Jo turned her attention to the car again, trying to keep her hands and new fine coral wool dress clear of any oil and grease, but in her heart she knew it was useless. She was going to have to ring the TV producer to cancel their appointment, but if she did that . . .

Several cars zoomed by, their drivers suddenly trans-fixed by some object of riveting interest on the far horizon. Huh! The age of chivalry is certainly dead round here, thought Jo ruefully. No chance of any of *them* helping out a damsel in distress. Of all the mornings, it just had to be today. She kicked the nearest tyre and leaned her head on her hand, tight-lipped, staring at the engine as though willing it into life.

She was too preoccupied to notice the silver-grey Aston Martin pull on to the verge behind her, or hear the footsteps.

'Jo?'

She jumped, and spun round to see Adam Roker standing just behind her.

'What on earth are you up to at this time of the morning?'

His faint smile, his easy assurance maddened her, caught as she was at a complete disadvantage.

'Oh, it was such a lovely morning, I decided to give the car engine a thorough overhaul,' she replied, ironically, conscious even as she spoke, of the thin drizzle settling on her hair and clothes.

'All right—I put it badly. What's wrong with your car?'

'If I knew that, I would hardly be standing here now, would I?' she retorted unreasonably, but he ignored her words and bent over the engine.

'Get in and try to start it while I check the leads and the distributor.'

'But I've——'

'Get in, Jo. I'm in a hurry.'

He took off his charcoal-grey jacket and tossed it on to the passenger seat. Then he fiddled around for some minutes while Jo sat tapping the steering-wheel and covertly watching him as, oblivious of her gaze, he worked on the car, frowning in concentration. A lock of dark hair fell forward over his brow and he brushed it aside impatiently, leaving a faint streak of oil. Finally, he looked up briefly.

'Try it now.'

She switched on hopefully but the engine only whined in protest.

Adam straightened up, wiping his hands. 'It's no go, I'm afraid.'

The hope which had risen in her with his arrival fizzled out. 'But you're an engineer, aren't you?' she demanded.

'I'm a petroleum engineer, not a garage mechanic—the two things do happen to be fairly dissimilar. Anyway, I know what's wrong with it—there's no spark from the points. And not only that—you've flooded it. You've been messing with the choke, I've no doubt.'

Temper, coupled with frustration, rose in a spiral within Jo. She banged her hands down on the steering-wheel, snatched up her handbag and jacket, got out and slammed the door so that the bonnet fell down, narrowly missing Adam, and the whole car quivered on its tyres. She turned on her heel to walk away, unable to trust her voice, but Adam blocked her path and put his hands on her wrists.

'You haven't told me where you're off to.'

She laughed, unable quite to keep the bitterness out of her tone. 'Back home, rather quicker than I'd intended.' When he looked questioningly at her, she hesitated then went on, 'Well, if you must know, I was going to London. I have—had—an appointment this morning with a TV producer to talk about Pear Trees being featured in the next series of that *Oaks From Acorns* programme.'

In spite of herself, she could not manage quite to hide her pride.

'But that's a business programme, isn't it?'

'Yes—they're hoping to do a feature on several up-and-coming small restaurants.'

Adam loosed his grip and opened the passenger door of the Aston Martin. 'Come on.'

'But—where are we going?' Jo was hanging back uncertainly.

'London, of course.' He glanced at her, then went on impatiently. 'Oh, don't worry. I'm not going out of my way—I've got a meeting there myself this morning.' He glanced at his watch, then added with a hint of irritation. 'And I'll be late for it if you don't stop clutching your throat like a terrified Victorian heroine—so *get in!*'

Sharing a car with Adam all the way to London? Sitting beside him? Making stilted conversation?

'Oh, no—thank you, but——'

'For God's sake, Jo.' He leaned his head down on his hand for a moment. '*I'm* going to London. *You're* going to London—by your own admission, for an important interview. I simply will not allow you to spite yourself in order to get at me. Either get in of your own accord or I'll pick you up and throw you in. You choose—now.'

Jo experienced one moment of impotent fury against the malignant fate which had first dumped Adam Roker back on her doorstep and had now put her well and truly in his power, then as he moved slightly towards her she climbed hastily in. He collected his jacket, locked her car, then got in beside her. But then, despite his impatience of a moment ago, he sat, idly tracing a pattern with his thumb on the steering-wheel.

'This TV programme—you said it's about Pear Trees, but surely they'll be featuring you pretty prominently. After all, the programme's about *people* in business—what makes them tick, and so on.'

'Well, yes, I suppose so.' Jo hadn't really considered this aspect. 'Yes, I imagine it will feature me to a certain extent, but I think they're planning to film down here, so Pear Trees will surely be the centre of attention.'

'You really are doing well, aren't you? I didn't realise

just how successful you were.' There was a flatness in his voice and it puzzled Jo, but when she looked at him, his eyes were still intent on the steering-wheel. So preoccupied was he with his thoughts that he seemed hardly aware that she was speaking. 'What did you say?'

'I said, you've got a smudge of oil on your forehead,' she said, trying to change the subject.

He reached into the glove pocket and Jo reluctantly took the tissue he held out to her. She concentrated all her attention on the oil streak, avoiding actually touching his skin with her fingers. She studied the spot critically and then, inevitably, her eyes met his. She looked away quickly, feeling her colour rise, and said, 'That's it, I think.'

'Fine—thanks.'

His arm brushed casually across her as he leaned across to unhook her seat belt.

'Quite comfortable, are you?' he asked as they drove off.

'Yes, thank you.' She stared out of the side window while ten miles flew past.

'Not cold are you? I can put the heater on.'

'Oh, no—no thank you. I'm fine.'

Another ten miles, and Jo began to recover her composure a little. She cleared her throat to speak just as Adam, his eyes on the road, said, 'And how are you, Jo?'

She shrugged. 'Oh, I'm OK.' Then, feeling that she was being too off-hand, she made an effort. 'You've been abroad?'

'Yes, I've been out in the Middle East for the last month or so.' There was a pause. 'How's Jon?'

'He's fine. He got his maths right, by the way.'

Adam laughed. 'Good—I wasn't too sure. This modern maths they go in for nowadays is a bit beyond me.'

'Well, thank you anyway. He——'

She broke off and he prompted her. 'Yes?'

'Oh—nothing.' She had been about to say that Jon had, for the first couple of weeks, driven her almost crazy asking, 'When's Adam coming again?' But she had to keep a strict watch on her tongue. She might be grateful for the lift, but there was no need to give him that satisfaction.

There was another pause, then Adam said, 'I suppose you know the deal's gone through? There are just a few loose ends to be tied up.'

A few loose ends, she thought. Like what happens to me and Pear Trees, I suppose. But she merely said, 'Look, Adam—I'd rather not talk about business at all today. Mark is handling everything at the Pear Trees end—I think it's better that way.'

She felt him shoot her a quick glance. 'Better?'

'Yes—surely you must agree that we should have as little contact as possible.'

He gave her another swift look and she knew he was frowning. For some reason, this infuriated her but she only clasped her hands more tightly in her lap.

'Jo—why won't you let us be friends? I'm not asking for anything more——' a hysterical laugh welled up deep inside her but she clamped it down '——but surely we can be friends?'

Jo stared out of the window, her mouth tight with anger. The countryside, just coming into its soft spring green, was beautiful and they were passing a wood, carved in two by the scar of the motorway, where there was a carpet of misty bluebells. But Jo did not see any of this. How dare he, how dare he? she raged inwardly. After all that he did to me—nearly destroyed me—and now he comes back and calmly says, can't we be friends?

Adam, glancing at her averted face, saw that she was even paler than usual and said, 'I mean it, Jo. We *can* be friends. After all, we were more—much more—than that to each other once, weren't we?'

His voice was soft, almost caressing. Jo's throat tightened frighteningly until she was panting for breath and she moved in her seat restlessly, trying to ward off the memories that his words evoked. He was right. They had once—for those few brief months—been the whole world to each other. And yes, in her innocent adoration, she had been totally, blissfully, happy—happier than she had ever been before or since. But that precious love, that fragile happiness, had been destroyed—destroyed by the man beside her—and it could never be reborn. With a strength born of pride she kept silent as he went on.

'I understand that you must feel badly about Pear Trees—not only how you think it should have come to you as of right, but also against us, as interlopers.'

She snatched at his words gratefully. Yes, that was it. Sidetrack him—let him think it was the threat to Pear Trees that was troubling her and he wouldn't suspect anything else.

She forced herself to give a hard laugh. 'Well, Adam, I'm glad you understand the situation. After all, you can hardly blame me for viewing you as—interlopers—and it really should have come to me, if there was any justice.' She deliberately infused a note of petulance into her voice then went on, 'And now let's drop it, shall we? This is the first time I've been away from Pear Trees—apart from trips to the kitchen suppliers—for months, so let me enjoy the novel experience.'

She forced a bright smile, then turned to study the passing scenery once more.

Adam pulled up outside the studios with ten minutes to spare and Jo smoothed back her hair with slightly unsteady hands.

'This really is important to you, isn't it?'

She was reaching for her coat and bag. 'What? Oh, yes—yes, it is. Thanks, Adam.' She turned to him and smiled. 'I really am very grateful.'

He didn't smile back. 'Good luck. If you're out before I get back, wait in the lobby for me.'

'Oh, no—that won't be necessary. I'll get myself something to eat, then there's a train from Paddington at——'

But he interrupted her wearily. 'Don't start that stupid nonsense again, Jo, please. My meeting will only be a short one. It's mainly a signing session—documents and so on. No, nothing about Pear Trees,' he added smoothly, as her eyes darkened. 'So be a good girl and sit tight—I'll be back for you.'

The discussion with the producer took longer than Jo had expected and therefore she was not in the least surprised to see Adam comfortably ensconced in an armchair in the lobby when she stepped out of the lift. As she walked across to him, her mood of elation was heightened by her amused awareness of the openly envious glances of the receptionists when he rose to greet her, and she felt their eyes still on them as he guided her out to the car.

Once they were inside he turned to her. 'Well? How did it go?' His voice was cool but there was tension behind the casualness.

'Oh, fine, just fine, thank you.' She tried to maintain her role as the sophisticated, blasé businesswoman, but her voice betrayed her bubbling excitement. 'We had a long chat about my training, about how Pear Trees has been built up over the last few years and so on and they seem to think it'll fit in well with the series. They hope to come down to do some filming later in the year.'

She smiled at him, her eyes bright and her cheeks flushed

a deep wild-rose pink, but he only said, rather sombrely, 'Good. I'm glad it went well. Now, how about something to eat?'

'Oh, no—no thanks. We had a tray of coffee and biscuits and besides——' she took a deep breath '——I'm just so excited, I don't think I could eat a thing.'

As Adam manoeuvred the car out of the car park, she leaned back in her seat happily watching the flow of lunchtime traffic, content to sit silent as he threaded the big car through one snarl of vehicles after another. She glanced at her watch and smiled with satisfaction. After all the worry and upset that morning, things could not have gone better—in fact, apart from the awkwardness of sitting in such close proximity to Adam for so long, things had actually been better. She would certainly not have been so relaxed at the studios if she had had to fight her way through the morning traffic into London, and now it looked as though she might even be home in time to pick Jon up from school, or at least to save Daphne the chore of getting his meal.

She had been idly watching the traffic signs, when all at once she blurted out, 'Hey, you've missed that turn to the motorway—it was signposted "M4, Reading and Swindon".'

'That's all right—we're not going back quite yet.'

'But—but we must. I've got to get home.' Her voice rose sharply.

'Keep calm—there's no hurry,' he said coolly, then as Jo started protesting, he went on quietly, 'Before my meeting, I rang the garage—they were going out to tow your car in later this morning—and then, while I was on the phone, I rang Pear Trees and spoke to a very pleasant woman— Daphne? She says you aren't to worry—she'll put Jon to bed and stay with him till you get back—and you're to be as late as you like. So that's all right then, isn't it?'

Jo, her face scarlet with temper, glared at him but he seemed quite oblivious of her feelings, his attention fully taken up with the traffic. She swallowed hard several times, digging her nails savagely into her palms. He glanced at her.

'What's the matter now?'

She was unable to contain her fury any longer.

'Oh, nothing—I was just counting up to five hundred before I dared trust myself to speak. Of all the—just because you've done me a favour today, that gives you no right to neatly organise my life behind my back as if—as if I *belonged* to you. I won't stand for it!'

Adam sighed dramatically. 'Why do some women always overreact?' he asked of no one in particular. 'Listen to me, Jo. You said yourself that you rarely get away from home. Surely, for you to be off the leash for just a few hours, instead of tearing back, in a panic in case you're not there to give Jon his tea for the first time in his life, isn't going to scar you for ever—or your son, either.'

'You leave Jon out of this.' Jo's voice had gone dangerously quiet. 'Now, turn the car round.'

'No.'

Jo's hand made an irresolute movement, as though to snatch at the wheel, then it dropped back in her lap. There was no point. The old Adam Roker had had a certain tone of voice, a curt decisiveness, which there had been no arguing with, and she had not seen anything in the new Adam to make her suspect that he had shed that particular character trait.

'Where did you think of going then?' she asked, her voice tinkling with ice. 'Brighton?'

'No—I don't think so. Let's see, where are we? Ah, Hampstead two miles. I tell you what, let's have a blow on the Heath—the fresh air will do us both good. That is, unless you've got any other suggestions?'

She jerked her head round, as though on a puppet string, but he was gazing casually straight ahead. He's forgotten, she told herself with one quick stab of bitterness, forgotten that the Heath was one of *our* places. But, after all, why shouldn't he—he's had no reason to remember, as I have, all these years. She thought grimly of how she had felt just a few minutes before—how it had *almost* seemed a good idea to have Adam chauffeur her to London. Now, she realised the truth. Her presence in the car alone with him was forcing her to admit memories long since buried and she felt the bitter-sweet recollections rise in her like gall, so that when the car stopped she plunged out straight away, as if to break through the web that was encircling her.

The wind upon the Heath was bracing, as though it had blown for miles over high moorland instead of through city streets, and Jo snuggled down into the collar of her navy jacket, glad of its warmth. She walked off quickly but when she heard Adam's footsteps behind her she slowed reluctantly. As he strode towards her, she sensed for a moment the tentacles of the past tugging at her mind, but then she shook herself free of their grasp.

Adam made no attempt to take her arm and they walked some way in silence. They passed a grey, bent little old woman, with three tiny dogs on leads made from string, and he said, 'An exiled Russian countess, I should think.'

'What?' She was startled out of her private thoughts.

He looked down at her. 'Don't tell me you've forgotten— surely you remember the game we played when we came here—how we used to make up stories about all the strange people we saw.'

Jo stood quite still as recollection flooded through her. A short while before, she had silently accused him of forgetting, but it was he who had remembered the private game they used to play—and she had long since forgotten it.

'Yes—yes, I remember,' she said in a voice tight with constraint, and she looked down at the grass, unwilling to meet his dark eyes. She gave a lopsided smile, still not looking at him. 'You were always much better at it than I was.'

'Oh well, I used to tell you that was just my eight years' seniority.'

'No you didn't—you always said it was because you were cleverer than me.' She stopped herself—this was utter folly. She began to scuff a circle with her toe in the dust, still unable to meet his eyes.

He put a hand on her arm. 'Jo——' he began, but she burst out fiercely,

'No, Adam, don't say anything—please don't say anything at all. I didn't want to come here today, and I'm certainly not going to rake over the ashes of the past. I told you—it's over and dead.' As his hand tightened on her arm she wrenched herself away from him. 'It's starting to rain—let's go back to the car.'

Adam loosed her arm with an angry gesture. 'All right, have it your way—we'll go back to the damned car!'

Before she could protest, he had seized her round the waist, drawing her to him so close that she could hardly breathe, her face half buried against the dark cloth of his coat.

'Adam—let me go—you're hurting me!' she gasped, as she was forced along, half running, half stumbling. 'Will—you—let—me—go!' She fought against him, until he stopped abruptly. The cold rain was pouring down their faces but there was no mistaking the pent-up anger in his eyes, just a few inches from her own, and Jo quailed before it.

'Shut up!' he snapped, then, crushing her to him even more fiercely, he half carried her towards the car, his face set. He unlocked her door but did not open it. Instead, he thrust her against the side of the car, so that she could feel his heart beating against her. Ignoring the rain streaming down their faces, he released the grip on her waist and wrenched her face up towards him.

She twisted her head desperately from side to side and gasped, 'Stop it! Stop it, Adam, or I'll——'

'Or you'll what?' he grated, and before she could move, his mouth came down hard on hers, silencing all her protests in a hard, angry kiss.

She met his anger with more. How could he do this—how dared he? His lips parted hers and she felt his tongue probing her mouth, hostile, demanding, taking possession of it. A sudden gust of stinging rain slapped at their faces, so that he involuntarily loosened his grip for a moment and she tore her mouth away from his. Fighting for self-control, she glared furiously up at him.

'Open the door, please—and do try to behave a little more like a gentleman, even if we both know you aren't one.'

She had the satisfaction of seeing his face flush with mortified anger as he pushed her into the car and threw himself in beside her, breathing heavily. They sat in silence as the rain trickled like tears down the windscreen then he tried, more gently this time, to turn her head towards him, but she would not look at him.

'Jo.'

'No, Adam.' Her voice was empty. 'You shouldn't have kissed me.'

He shrugged. 'You've seemed so—offhand, so untouchable, ever since I met you again. I suddenly felt that I had to break through that mask to the real you.'

'But there is no mask. This is the real me.' Her voice was expressionless. 'Offhand, untouchable ... I've told you, that other girl—if she ever existed—disappeared long ago.'

'Maybe I wanted to prove to myself that she hasn't really gone—at least, for ever.'

'Oh, but she has, Adam, believe me—and I should know. You'll save yourself a great deal of trouble if you accept that simple fact.'

She turned to him, to emphasise her words, and saw with disbelief that his expression was strained, almost sad. Had he really thought that she would allow him to walk nonchalantly back into her life and start exactly where he had left off? Yes, he obviously had. And why should this be so surprising—it was perfectly in keeping with his male arrogance and self-assurance. As her anger simmered again, she realised he was speaking.

'I do understand how you feel about me. Don't think I don't feel badly——'

He broke off, his mouth tight, and Jo, her stomach lurching with apprehension, burst out, 'No, Adam—don't go on!'

'But, even so, surely you needn't have reacted quite so badly—gone over the top quite so much—at just one kiss, even from me.'

'Tell me this,' Jo snapped, her face very pale. 'Just why do you think I should want your kisses—or anyone else's? I don't need them—I don't need any man's kisses!'

The savagery of her words startled them both and Adam remained silent for a moment.

'Come now, Jo,' he said at last, his voice hard. 'Don't let's get hypocritical. You're a very attractive young woman, even if you've done your best to turn yourself into an ice-maiden as far as I'm concerned. Don't try and tell me you've been living under a vow of chastity for the last eight years. I don't know how many men there have been, of course——'

'How many——' In spite of her anger, the astonished laugh bubbled out before she could prevent it.

'What's the matter? Did I say something amusing?'

'Oh, no—not at all. It's just that—well, having been closeted at Pear Trees for most of that time, I'd hate you to think I'd been enjoying one torrid relationship after another.' She couldn't quite succeed in keeping the bitterness out of her voice.

Too late, she realised that it might have been better to let him think she had been doing just that and why, in any case, should she care a fig for his good opinion?

'One, surely, though.' His voice was curt.

'What? Oh, you mean Mark. He's just——'

'No—I did not mean him. Surely you haven't forgotten?'

'Forgotten who?'

'Jon's father.' His voice was flat, toneless. 'Did he mean so little to you? Surely it was more than just a one-night stand?'

Sick outrage exploded in her and she stared at him, white-faced, her eyes blazing green with anger. 'How dare you, Adam Roker! You force your way back into my life— nobody asked you to—then you—oh, it's too ridiculous!'

'Why is it so ridiculous?' His eyes were stern, probing her, and Jo pulled herself together, realising that her tongue had almost carried her away. After all, it was a million times better for him to think that of her than to know the truth. Ignoring his question, she took a deep breath to steady herself.

'I'm not prepared to continue this conversation any longer,' she said coldly. 'As I told you before—you forfeited all right to tell me how to behave when you did your disappearing act.'

'You've got your facts a bit twisted, haven't you? Surely it was you who did the disappearing?'

'That's a matter of opinion,' she snapped and then, as he flushed angrily, she went on decisively, 'Anyway, I refuse to talk about it any more and if you try to, I swear I'll get out of the car and walk. Now—can we please go home?'

'Not just yet—but don't worry, the subject's closed.' He started up the engine and reversed savagely out of the parking space.

'Where are we heading for now?' Jo asked, her voice strained.

'You're soaked through and I don't want you going down with double pneumonia—you'd no doubt say it was my fault. So I'm taking you somewhere where you can dry off and have a hot bath.'

He drove on without speaking to her again and Jo stared out of the passenger window, letting the busy city scenes flow over her, distracting her just a little from her disturbing thoughts. The car finally stopped in a quiet, tree-lined street, outside an imposing, double-fronted red-brick Edwardian house. Beside the white painted front door was a row of gleaming brass plates and on one, in bold lettering, Jo read 'ADAM ROKER'.

CHAPTER FIVE

'You live here!' Jo exclaimed.

His laugh was quite genuine.

'That's right—got it in one. You knew I lived in London.
What sort of place did you think I'd have—a bench on the
Embankment?'

Adam's flat occupied the whole of the third floor. He
unlocked the door and gestured her in.

'Welcome to my humble bachelor pad.'

But there was nothing humble about this particular pad,
Jo realised, after a few moments' inspection—just a great
deal of solid comfort, in the tweed wool carpet and the suite
of beige upholstered leather. Even so, the room was faintly
impersonal, even austere, almost like a monk's cell, she
thought. The only individual touches were a couple of
beaten copper jugs, with a Middle Eastern look to them,
and on the stone hearth a large abstract shape in pale wood,
while along one wall there were several modern prints,
from which the stark male figures stared out at her
uncompromisingly.

While Adam lit the gas fire, she crossed to one of the two
square sash windows and stood studying the length of the
street below, feeling thoroughly ill at ease. Her mouth was
dry and there was an odd, butterflies feeling in her
stomach. When Adam had arrived at Pigsties she had, after
the initial shock, been at least outwardly in control of
herself—after all, she was on her own territory. But now,
really alone with him, in *his* flat, she felt unaccountably
nervous.

Adam straightened up and crossed the room to her, seemingly unaware of her feelings. He took her unwilling hand for a moment, then dropped it. 'You're frozen—you'd better get out of those wet things and have a hot bath or you'll be ill.'

Jo glanced down at her jacket and dress and saw with astonishment that they were sodden, and when she wriggled her toes in her beige leather shoes her feet squelched. She began reluctantly to take off her jacket.

'Oh, I'll just sit by the fire. I'll be all right—I'm tough.'

'We all know how tough you are,' he said, unsmiling, 'but I'm not giving you the option. I'll go and run a bath for you.'

When he had gone, Jo went over to the fire and sat down on the rug, as near to the flickering gas flames as she could without setting light to herself. She felt chilled all through and her teeth were chattering—and not only with cold. She smoothed out her dress and held her wet feet towards the warmth; she might be able to dry them before he returned.

When he came back, a quarter of an hour later, she was sitting with her knees up under her chin, her arms wrapped around them. He came over to her and, putting his hands under her elbows, lifted her easily to her feet.

'I'm all right,' she insisted. 'My feet are dry now and so's my dress—well, almost,' she added, seeing the steam rising gently from it.

Adam shook her impatiently by the arms. 'You're shivering. You need a hot bath and you're having one. No! No more arguments—unless you want me to undress you and bath you myself!'

'N-no, I'll go,' said Jo, hastily backing away from him.

'That's better. You'll find a dressing-gown in the spare bedroom, through there. Take as long as you like—I've got plenty of work to be getting on with.'

Without another word, Jo retreated into the other room, undressed and went through to the bathroom, which was large and luxurious in a solid, old-fashioned sort of way—a huge, deep bath and dark mahogany fittings. Adam had put out a pile of fluffy pink towels and on the side of the bath was a large bottle of French bath oil. She poured some into the water and the deliciously rich scent of carnations filled the room. She hung her dress and tights near the heated towel rail and got into the bath. The hot, scented water lapped round her chilled body, seeping into her taut muscles, relaxing her overstretched nerves and, almost against her own volition, she eased herself back into its soothing heat and closed her eyes.

She stayed in the bath for half an hour or more, running hot water as it cooled, until every bit of the chill and aching tension had melted out of her body. There was another door leading from the bathroom and she heard Adam moving about and then retreat into the sitting-room. When she had patted herself dry she could not resist a peep into what was clearly his bedroom. She withdrew her head guiltily but then, wrapping herself in the towel, she crept in, her heart pattering, her feet soundless over the high-pile brown carpet.

The furniture was of smooth, matt teak; there was a set of silver-backed brushes and combs on the dressing-table. The bed itself was a large double one, and was covered by an Indian woven rug in shades of brown, cream and black. A modern still life painting in oils; a book on the bedside table—these were the only signs of occupation, but all the same, Adam's presence was overwhelming and Jo felt herself to be an intruder on his privacy.

Clutching the towel to her, she had turned to retreat from the room when she noticed the photograph. It was in a heavy silver frame on the low window-sill and she picked it up. The central figure—a plump, dark-haired young woman in denim dungarees—was smiling fondly down at the man who was sprawled on the grass at her feet. Jo's heart skipped a beat. Adam was barely recognisable for the two small boys spreadeagled across his chest, while behind him a pink-smocked toddler was busy pulling his hair out by the roots. It was a happy, joyful scene and Jo could almost hear the shrieks of childish glee. As she stared, wide-eyed, at the photograph, she was suddenly struck by an acute stab of pain, which took her totally unawares. Surely—surely she couldn't possibly be feeling jealous of this pretty woman with her carefree children!

Thrusting the thought from her, Jo quietly replaced the photograph and went back through to the spare room. She picked up the towelling wrap from the bed and as she put it on she realised that it was not Adam's, as she had assumed—it would never have fitted him—but a woman's. It was a couple of sizes too large for her, but was a woman's nonetheless. There was even a faint, not unpleasant, whiff of stale perfume on the collar as she slipped into it.

The wardrobe door was slightly ajar and Jo, driven by a sudden burning desire to *know*, looked inside. There were two or three blouses hanging up, one of them a pink satin evening blouse, a couple of skirts—good quality by the feel of them—and a pair of very high-heeled black evening shoes. Jo closed the wardrobe door noiselessly and went back to the bathroom. She opened the cabinet door and saw, as she somehow knew she would, female toiletry articles—a make-up bag, small electric hair tongs, deodorant, and a tin of expensive carnation body talc. She had raised her eyebrows slightly when she smelt the very feminine bath oil—now she knew the explanation. Adam's own few bottles were lined up on the bottom shelf in a neat orderly row.

Jo closed the cabinet door and sat down on the edge of the bath, staring into space, her mind racing erratically. Was Adam married, after all? He had told her he wasn't—had even hinted that his memories of her had got in the way. No, surely not—no woman married to Adam would be content to have him live in his 'pad' in London . . . He must be having an affair. Yes, that was it. They might even be planning to marry when her divorce came through . . . That, at least, was all to the good. It would surely get Adam out of her hair for good and all. And why on earth shouldn't he marry? She had Jon and Pear Trees—that was quite enough for her. But there was no reason why Adam's work should be enough to fill *his* whole life. Good luck to him— she hoped they would both be happy!

The children . . . no wonder he was so good with Jon. As her thoughts strayed back to the scene in the photograph, incredulously she became aware of another completely unexpected emotion—a treacherous but inescapable pang of guilt. She rejected it fiercely, but all the same it left her momentarily shaken. Why on earth should she have the slightest feelings of remorse for the way she had behaved towards Adam? By his callous treatment of her, he deserved nothing better from her. But none the less, it was a fact that she had willingly connived at depriving him of all knowledge of his own child—and, what was more, had every intention of continuing to do so.

She paused in the sitting-room doorway. Adam, who had changed into slim-fitting beige cords and a black fine-knit rollneck sweater, was sitting at his desk, littered with papers, his back half turned to her. As she hesitated, he ran his fingers through his hair in an impatient gesture which, for a heart-stopping moment, took her back to the days of that far-off summer when she would tiptoe up behind him as he worked and put her hands over his eyes. But there could be no question of that now ...

Adam, as if sensing her presence, glanced round.

'Good—the dressing-gown fits. I was afraid it would be enormous on you—you're so skinny now.'

She didn't rise to the bait but merely replied, 'Well, it's a bit big but I'm quite comfortable in it, thank you.'

Her voice was stilted but he did not seem to notice. He shuffled the papers together, pushed back his chair and came towards her. Jo, conscious that under the robe she was naked, tensed in every muscle but he merely took her hand for a moment.

'Ah, that's better. You're a little less like a half-frozen sparrow now.'

He glanced at the small brass carriage clock on the low mantelpiece. 'Now—food. There's an excellent little French bistro round the corner—or I'll make us a meal here. And don't look like that.' He shook his head reprovingly. 'All you good cooks are the same—think no one else can butter a piece of bread.'

Jo smiled. 'No, I wasn't thinking that, I promise you. I was just going to say that I'm still not at all hungry, so if you could just do a couple of toasted sandwiches, I'd rather have that than go out for a full-scale meal, thanks all the same.'

When he had gone, she sank down on the hearthrug, feeling the cosy warmth of the room wrap itself around her. She leaned back against the armchair and picked up the wooden carving, letting her fingers play idly over the smooth pale surface, as she listened to the subdued clatterings from the other side of the door. She would have liked to go out and offer her help, but instinctively she knew that Adam would not wish it.

She came to with a start, to find Adam standing over her, holding knives, forks and two wine-glasses. She stared up at him for a moment and he misunderstood her expression.

'Look, Jo—let's have a truce, just for today. OK? Surely we're both old enough—to forget the past, aren't we—at least for a few hours?'

Jo felt the old resentment stir in her at his seemingly casual words but, mellowed by the bath and the warmth, she could not work up any real hostility and she nodded.

'I just want you to—well, enjoy the rest of the day. In spite of my company, of course—which you obviously don't find very pleasurable.'

He squatted down on his haunches beside her, so that she was uncomfortably aware of his body, the almost animal vitality that he still exuded, and shrank back, her fingers tightening on the carving on her lap.

'This—this is beautiful.'

'Yes—it's an abstract of a mountain lion. I saw it last week in a *souk* in Rabbaq and couldn't resist it.'

'So you've been out to Rabbaq?'

'Yes—I've managed to keep up my ties there over the last few years. In fact, I often think I'm happiest there—out in the desert, working on the new oil-field they're developing, getting filthy and sweaty.' He pulled a rueful face. 'So you see, Jo, the sleek, debonair business tycoon you see before you is just a sham!'

'In that case, why on earth have you got yourself involved with the syndicate?'

He shrugged. 'Oh, it's all part of my long-term plan for the advancement of Adam Roker! I made a fair bit of money from my first spell in Rabbaq and used it to make some well-placed investments in the City. I met up with Giles—who, by the way, is a much shrewder operator than I might have suggested; practically everything he touches is guaranteed to turn into solid platinum—and he asked me to join the consortium he was building up.'

'So things have worked out for you just as you'd always intended?'

'Pretty well, yes.' The bantering tone had gone from his voice. 'Not quite in every way, of course—but you can't expect to win them all.'

She looked up, straight into his eyes, inches away from hers, and he held her gaze so that she was unable to break free.

'Jo?'

His voice was husky and he lifted his hand as though to touch her, but she jerked away and he got to his feet, his face blank once more.

'Dinner is served. Have it by the fire if you like.'

When he set down the tray she gave a gasp of horror. 'Steak! I can't manage that—I told you, just a sandwich,' she almost wailed.

But in fact, once she started to eat she realised that, in spite of her protests, she was ravenous. The steak was meltingly tender, the chips crisp and golden, the dressing for the salad home-made. She glanced at Adam and his eyes glinted with amusement.

'I told you I wouldn't poison you. And if you ask me, you could do with a few more meals like this—you might lose a bit of your waif-and-stray look.'

'I suppose so. I imagine it's always being surrounded by food at Pear Trees. I very rarely seem to be hungry.'

He held up the bottle of Bordeaux. 'More wine?'

'No thanks—one glass is plenty.'

He cleared away the plates and came back in a few minutes with two glass dishes piled high with raspberries and cream.

'Oh, Adam, you're spoiling me!' she exclaimed.

'They're frozen, I'm afraid, but they're usually quite good, even so. As for spoiling—well, you could do with some of that, I think, don't you?' She turned her head away and he went on, 'You're like me, Jo—you didn't grow up on the sunny side of the wall, but now you're a big girl and the sunshine's there, you know—that's if you're determined enough to find it. Everybody should spoil themselves sometimes—even if it's only with supermarket frozen raspberries!' He spoke lightly enough but his expression was serious.

Later, she insisted on helping with the washing up in the kitchen, which was functional and uncluttered, as she had known it would be. Her clothes had dried, so she dressed, hastily combed out her bedraggled hair into its usual smooth knot, then returned to the sitting-room, where Adam was packing away his papers into a slim attaché case.

'By the way,' he said, 'I didn't tell you—that dress is rather fetching. It suits you.'

'Thank you.' She smoothed down the folds of wool, then in an effort to break the tension that suddenly hung in the air between them, she pulled a face. 'I made it myself, so I only hope my mistakes don't show—or that it doesn't start to unravel!'

'You made it yourself! Don't you ever let up? You're a workaholic, Jo—just what are you trying to prove?'

The severity in his voice surprised her and she hesitated, then said, 'Well—actually, I wanted something special for this morning and I couldn't afford to buy it. No, it's true,' she went on quickly, seeing his disbelief, 'I know Pear Trees is doing well and looks, well, affluent, but almost every penny I make, apart from keeping myself and Jon, is ploughed back. My aunt was heavily in debt to the bank when she died,' she ended, almost defiantly.

'I didn't know,' he said slowly. 'I'd assumed—well, I'm surprised Sinclair didn't tell me.'

'He probably thought it might weaken our position in

any bargaining we might get involved in—and maybe I shouldn't have told you.'

'Oh, our accountants would have ferreted it out. But I appreciate your telling me—seeing that I'm one of the enemy, so to speak. In any case, it won't make any difference, Jo—we've definitely decided to hang on to the whole estate, including Pear Trees and your piece of land. But there's no reason at all, as far as I can see, why you can't continue, if you want to, just as before.'

'No—no reason at all. Although if you really think we can carry on exactly as before, with your precious wonderland just the other side of the hedge——' She broke off, biting her lip. 'I—I'm sorry. I won't say any more. You've got your job to do. I quite understand—really, I do.'

She caught up her bag and jacket. 'I think we'd better go, don't you?'

In her ear, a voice was saying, 'Wake up, Jo. We're nearly there.'

She roused herself, to find that her head was lolling against Adam's shoulder and she jerked it away quickly.

'Sorry. I haven't been very good company on the way home, but I was up at five this morning.'

'Up at five? What on earth for?'

'Oh, I often am—to go into the market. It's better to do that than rely on a wholesaler. Bobbie and Phil take turns sometimes, but they need their beauty sleep. Anyway, just wait till the asparagus season—I'll be off up to Evesham by four. And don't start lecturing me again—I enjoy it, honestly. I wouldn't do anything else, if I could.'

He grunted a reply as he drove through the village street and as they pulled into the gateway of Pear Trees Jo yawned luxuriously. 'Thank you, Adam—for the meal— and for helping out today. I really am grateful.'

'My pleasure.'

She hesitated a moment then thought, after all, it won't hurt to be 'civilised' just this once, and said, 'Would you like to come in for a coffee? It's been a long drive.'

'Well, if you're sure you're not too tired. Just five minutes, then.'

They got out of the car and Jo took a deep breath of the clear air. At the front door, she fumbled in her bag for the key, but as she did so a light appeared in the hall and the door was flung open. Daphne stood there, pale and distraught.

'Oh, Jo, thank heavens you're back—I thought you were never coming!'

Jo's hand went to her throat. 'Why? What's happened? Where's Jon?' she demanded, almost frozen with terror.

Jon answered her himself. He burst out of the sitting-room, his tear-stained face contorted with fury. Launching himself at his mother, he hugged her convulsively as he screamed out, 'Where were you? I wanted you—I wanted you! I hate Daphne—I hate her! I wanted you to put me to bed, not her.'

He banged his head against her breast, utterly beside himself with passion. Jo, her face like paper, tried to restrain him but he was too strong for her and his flailing arms caught her a savage blow on the mouth so that she loosed her grip. She had totally forgotten Adam's presence and when she became aware of Jon being lifted away from her by strong hands, for a second, in her confusion, she thought it was Daphne. Then she heard Adam's voice—calm, unruffled, soothing.

Jon, in a blind fury, turned on him, kicking and punching, but Adam just lifted the child off the ground and gathered him to his chest. He held him firmly until, after what seemed to Jo like half an eternity, the struggles stopped, Jon leaned his head against Adam's shoulder and began to cry, but quietly this time. Adam stood calmly rocking him backwards and forwards, until he gave a shuddering sigh and relaxed.

'Come on, old son—you've had a long day. Let's get you up to bed.' Adam's voice was gentle and Jon, with a last hiccough, nodded drowsily and snuggled down into his arms.

As soon as he had been carried off upstairs, Daphne began, 'Oh, Jo, I'm sorry, I really am. I've ruined your day—and you looked so happy when I opened the door.'

Her eyes were bright and Jo cut her short—she couldn't face any more tears. 'It's all right, Daphne—it's not your fault. You must have had a terrible time with him. And now we must get you back home—I'll drive you.'

Ignoring Daphne's protests, Jo insisted on running her home to her small, neat cottage at the far end of the village. When she got back, a quarter of an hour later, the only light was coming from the sitting-room. As she wearily pushed open the door she saw that Adam had made a start on clearing the room of Jon's toys. At first, she didn't see him, then realised he was standing over by the window, his back to her. He had drawn back the curtain and was staring out into the blackness.

Jo swallowed hard. Her pride—and shame—demanded that she ignore the scene with Jon as though it had never happened, but she made herself speak.

'I'm sorry,' she said huskily. 'He—he isn't very often like that—in fact, I've never seen him as bad as that before.'

Adam swivelled round towards her and she quailed before his bleak, stony look.

'Sit down, Johanna.'

She sank down on the sofa, her legs weak and trembling. 'It isn't his fault,' she began but he silenced her with a look. She watched as he walked over to the coffee-table and picked up a book. He dropped it on her lap and sat down heavily opposite her. She glanced at it then looked at him, a frown of puzzlement creasing her brow, then she looked back at the book.

'Oh, it's Jon's favourite. I——'

'Open it.'

Obediently, yet with a chill unease, Jo opened the cover. Her own handwriting leapt up off the page at her: 'To Jonathan, on his seventh birthday' and a date a few months previous. Underneath, Jon had written in his childish capitals: 'JONATHAN ADAM THORNTON, PIGSTIES COTTAGE, COMPTON LYDIATT, ENGLAND, EUROPE, THE WORLD. AGE SEVEN.'

She sat staring at it, thinking how strange it was that something as trivial as a child's story book should, in the end, have betrayed her so completely.

'He's mine, isn't he? Jonathan is my son.'

CHAPTER SIX

Jo closed the book and carefully replaced it on the coffee-table, giving herself a few precious moments to think. But what was there to think of? There was no escape—the evidence was there in black and white.

She looked up, trying to hold his eyes fearlessly, but quailed before the implacable anger she saw there. 'Yes, he's your son.'

Her words dropped like a pebble in the silence and she sat staring at her hands, thinking, if only—if only the car hadn't broken down . . . if only I hadn't gone to London . . . for the sake of five fleeting minutes on a TV programme, my whole life is ruined . . .

'Why?'

She gazed up at him, her eyes dark with exhaustion. 'Why what?'

He spread his hands in a gesture of impatience. 'Why did you do it to me—deny me my son for seven years? God, Johanna, I never realised you hated me so much.'

'*I* hated *you*? That's rich, coming from you!' Deep down inside her a bubble of laughter welled up until it burst out from her lips. She put her hands up to her mouth, hearing someone laughing. Adam's hands were gripping her shoulders, his fingers digging into her flesh as he shook her.

'Stop it, Jo! Stop it—you'll wake him up!'

That sobered her, so that she stopped laughing and stared at him. Abruptly, he released his grip and straightened up. 'I think we can both do with a drink.'

She gestured towards the sideboard and he fetched out a

82

full bottle of brandy and two glasses. He poured out a generous measure in each and handed one to her.

She sipped it, her teeth chattering against the rim, as he lowered himself into a chair, took a gulp of his drink and set down the glass.

'Now, tell me please, Jo—I must know.' He spoke very quietly but she could sense the tension within him. 'Why did you do it—keep Jon from me? And what did you mean—coming from me, that's rich?'

She looked across the width of the hearthrug at him and, disbelievingly, saw pain, even reproach, in his eyes. A wave of anger swept through her.

'Just how hypocritical can you get?' she exclaimed. 'Don't you try to come the hand-on-heart innocent with me—it won't work, I swear it won't.' All the old humiliation and heartbreak was flooding back, sweeping aside her caution and reserve. 'Why did I keep Jon from you?' Her voice was hot with hostility. 'Tell me this—how could I have done otherwise, when you walked off and left me, without a word of goodbye? I kept thinking— hoping—you'd ring me, come to me, write to me— anything.' Her voice quivered slightly but she steadied it. 'But no—off without a word. You said you loved me better than all the world, and then when I needed you——' she stopped, fearing her voice would betray her, then went on, 'Please go, Adam. It's over—it was over a long time ago. I don't ever want to set eyes on you again.'

Adam came and sat beside her on the sofa. He took her hand but she snatched it away. 'Jo, listen to me.'

She shook her head impatiently. 'No, I don't want to hear any excuses—they'll be pretty good, I've no doubt. After all, you've had nearly eight years to think of them. You must understand and accept it when I say—I've made a new life for myself *and* Jon. You're no part of it, and never will be.'

'Jo—you *must* listen to me. I swear I'll sit on this sofa until you do.'

She closed her eyes wearily. 'Well, what is it? Say it and go.'

'Whatever you've got fixed in your mind—and I'm beginning to have nasty suspicions about what's been going on—I'm going to tell you what really happened. Don't interrupt me, please—I'm going to tell you, and I swear to you on my life that every word will be the truth.'

He stopped, as though waiting for her to object, but she merely shrugged and said coolly, 'OK—tell me, then. Let's hear your version.'

'It isn't *my* version. It's the truth.' He tossed back his brandy but went on holding the empty glass, running a finger slowly round the rim. 'First of all, I didn't lie to you. I did love you—fell for you like a ton of bricks the first time I set eyes on you. In fact, looking back, I loved you too much. You were very young—just seventeen—and you couldn't cope—I think I nearly scared the life out of you.'

Jo moved restlessly on the sofa, feeling the old wound begin to tear ever so slightly at the edges. It was true. She had tried to hide it from him, but she had found it difficult to accept the almost frightening intensity of his passion for her.

Adam went on slowly, 'Things might have been all right, I think, although I knew that once *she* got you back down here she would do her best to kill any feelings you had for me. Then, a month before I finished my research I had that marvellous offer to go out to the Middle East—to Rabbaq—for three years—so good, there was no way I could have turned it down. A start like that was just what I had to have—surely you remember, Jo, I was desperately hard up.'

She sat motionless, remembering, as the wound opened up a little more. 'But you were so pliable, so trusting. I knew that as soon as you went home you would come under your aunt's spell again and I would lose you. Not only was she anti-men in general, she was certainly anti-Roker in particular. I was a penniless nobody—not good enough for her wonderful niece. Oh yes, I knew she felt like that—and she was right, of course, at that time. In fact, in one way, I'm actually grateful to her. I was already ambitious, but she honed my ambition and aggression—I was determined to show her.'

He glanced at her but Jo, very pale, was leaning back, her eyes closed. 'So I wanted you to marry me at once, present her with a *fait accompli*, and come out to Rabbaq with me. But you wouldn't. You went on and on about how you couldn't let her down, how she'd done everything for you, how she wanted you to go into the restaurant which she'd just started to build up. You swore that if I waited a few years you'd marry me, but I knew it would never happen, once you came home to her.'

Jo shook her head. 'I know you didn't trust me, Adam, but I would have done—I loved you very much. You never really knew me, after all, did you?' She gave him a sad little smile, then turned her head away. She closed her eyes for a few moments, unable to see the present for the past—that wonderful, sunlit summer with Adam . . . she, unable ever to walk sedately, running to meet him, to be swept up into his arms . . . wandering hand in hand through Kew Gardens on those balmy June evenings—once having to climb over a fence because they had stayed so long that the gates were shut . . . venturing into the intimidating library where he worked all day and sitting beside him, supposedly learning basic French sauces, but in reality doing her best to distract him—passing him little notes—until, half indulgent, half exasperated, he banished her to the next table . . .

'I'm not very proud of myself over the next bit.' Adam's voice was rough with emotion. 'Particularly not now that I know——' His mouth tightened. 'But I was desperate. I felt I couldn't live without you for three years—and then lose you for ever.'

As though he couldn't sit still any longer, he sprang up and leaned against the window frame, his back to her. 'I thought long and hard, and it seemed to me that your aunt had all the trump cards—except one.' His tone was detached, almost clinical. 'Because I knew that you could never contemplate a casual affair, I thought that— perhaps—a sexual relationship might bind you to me, and that you would then agree to marry me. So, the last night of term, when you were going home the next day, at the disco I deliberately plied you with alcohol—I drank a fair bit myself—to help me through with it, I suppose.'

He stopped and there was silence in the room, then as he turned to face her, a smile of grim self-mockery flickered across his face. 'I was arrogant enough to think that I might even make it so marvellous for you . . . But in the event—it didn't quite work out that way.'

He looked down at her, willing her to meet his eyes, but Jo only gave an involuntary shudder. For so many years, she had forced the memory of that dreadful night far away from her conscious mind, had built a wall like a dam to keep it securely in the innermost recesses of her being. Now, at Adam's words, the wall heaved and cracked and the dam burst as the memories spewed out . . .

. . . The flickering lights, the blaring music . . . after one drink, she felt happy, happier than she had been all day. She refused another but Adam merely stood looking down, not at her but at her empty glass for several seconds, a strange expression on his face, then snatched it up, telling her it was more orange than anything else. That second drink made her feel even more relaxed, so that she willingly had another, until the throbbing ache of sadness over their parting was quite blotted out by the onslaught of alcohol, music and lights ... It didn't even seem strange that it was Adam's room, not her own, that she was in; his bed that she was collapsing on to, dizzy and unsteady ...

At first, in her deep love, she had welcomed him, embracing and holding him close. But then, as she saw his eyes blazing, his flushed face almost that of a stranger, and felt the naked urgency of his body, the treacherous fumes of alcohol cleared from her brain, love turned to panic—to terror—and she fought against him wildly ... There were no words of soft endearment, just her name over and over again in a kind of moan ... and then the final act of possession when, his face anguished, he cried, 'Forgive me, Jo!' before blotting out her cry of pain with his mouth and then lay, spent, on her rigid body ...

Jo huddled into the sofa, her eyes tightly shut, trying vainly to keep out the scenes which tumbled pell-mell through her mind ... She was lying dull-eyed, staring at the flickering neon signs reflected on the ceiling, while Adam lay, as if drugged, beside her until at last, just before dawn, she too dropped into a heavy sleep.

She finally came to, roused by the noise of traffic, and rolled over, her head thumping, for a few seconds quite unaware of where she was. Then, as she half-opened her eyes, realisation swept through her. As she looked down at her naked body, she saw the marks of Adam's fingers splayed across one arm and a bruise, faintly purple, on one breast. Hot colour flooded all over her and she pulled the sheet up tightly round her. Then she registered that she was quite alone—there was no sign of Adam. She felt utterly bewildered: not only her body, but her whole being was bruised by his assault.

A door banged nearby and she recoiled instantly, flinching deeper under the bedclothes. But Adam did not appear, and it gradually dawned on her that the tiny flat was silent. Gingerly, she sat up, her eyes half closed against the bright light pouring in through the flimsy curtains. Her clothes had been draped over a chair and she fumbled herself into them with shaking hands. Then she opened the door and peeped out. The wide landing was deserted, but from behind closed doors several radios were in strident competition, a baby was screaming, and there was a greasy smell of frying bacon which made Jo's stomach heave.

She closed the door and leaned against it. Adam had left—gone to the university, just as usual, as though nothing had happened—had not even waited for her to wake up. How could he when, as never before, she wanted him to be there, to reassure her that last night was a dream—a dreadful nightmare—and that everything was just as it had been. But she knew, with a devastating certainty, that for them nothing could ever be the same again.

Jo felt a sudden, overwhelming need to escape—away from the flat, away from Adam. In her distraught state, she needed time to get her thoughts together. There was only one place, one person, she could turn to.

She would tell Adam—yes, that was it—she would leave him a note to say that she had gone home, as planned. In that way, she would give herself the breathing space she so desperately needed to sort out her tumultuous feelings before Adam came to her once more. She left the note propped up on the window sill and let herself out of the flat.

In her anxiety to be gone, she took a taxi to the hostel where her cases were ready packed, then on to Paddington, where she just caught a mid-morning train . . .

. . . At Pear Trees, she waited . . . At first, she haunted the house. The phone rang that first day, when she was unpacking, and she flew downstairs. But Aunt Joan was just replacing the receiver. 'Only another wrong number, dear,' she smiled, with mock irritation. Tears of disappointment sprang to Jo's eyes and she almost blurted out her story but something—her loyalty to Adam perhaps—held her back.

But then, as days went by with no word, Jo, increasingly aware of her aunt's keen glances on her, took to wandering aimlessly for hours in the manor grounds, or lying in the lush meadow grass by the stream, staring unseeingly at the clouds. Each time, when she tentatively asked if there had been a phone call for her, Aunt Joan would reply, 'No, were you expecting one?' and she would stammer hastily, 'Oh, no—not really.' Each night she lay awake for hours, then overslept, and each morning her spirits lifted as she thought, today, today a letter will have come.

One morning, after nearly a week, she slept so late that her aunt brought her breakfast in bed. As she sat up, the phone rang but when she moved instinctively to get out of bed Aunt Joan firmly pushed her back and went downstairs. Half fearful, half excited, Jo was pushing her cereal round the dish when her aunt came back. She could only say, without lifting her eyes, 'Who—who was it?' and her aunt replied, 'Oh, just the builder about repairing the roof.' Jo, her stomach lurching with disappointment, put down her spoon and pushed the tray away. She lay down and closed her eyes, before the tears which were blurring her vision could spill over.

It was that same afternoon that Aunt Joan told Jo, her

voice brisk, that she had just rung her old friend, Madame Rocher, who ran a small hotel and restaurant in south Brittany, and Madame had jumped at the chance to have Jo's help over the next few months.

'It's a marvellous chance for you, Jo, to finish off your training. You'll be able to put into practice all those basic French sauces you had such trouble with,' she added teasingly. 'Besides, you deserve a holiday.'

Dazed and unprotesting, Jo looked on as her aunt booked the ferry passage and washed and repacked her clothes. Deep inside her a knell had been sounding with ever-increasing clamour, 'He isn't coming, he doesn't love you, doesn't love you,' and so this sudden, bewildering activity came almost as a relief.

Leaning over the ferry rail she blew her aunt a last kiss and shouted, 'See you at Christmas.' But, of course, it had not been Christmas, for within a few weeks Madame Rocher's sharp black eyes had registered as a certainty what Jo had resolutely refused to admit even as the remotest possibility . . .

'Jo, listen to me.' With a supreme effort, she tore herself out of the past, as Adam came and sat beside her. She saw that under his suntan he was very pale. 'I know I did you a great wrong. You were so very young, you trusted me and I—I betrayed your trust. But you must surely know—it was only because I loved you so much. But in the end it didn't matter, because I lost anyway.'

'You *loved* me?' Jo's voice was hard with anger. 'You expect me to believe that—when you couldn't even be bothered to wait for me to wake up that morning! You just went off, leaving me on my own!'

'Went off?' He was frowning at her in seemingly genuine puzzlement. 'Now, let's get this straight, Jo. I didn't just go off. When I woke up that morning you were asleep beside me, the tear marks still on your cheeks. I felt like drowning myself—I wanted to hold you, cherish you for ever.' He gave her the faintest smile, which she completely ignored, then went on jerkily, 'But after what had happened, I wasn't sure that you could ever bear for me to touch you again. So I decided to get you breakfast instead.

'A couple of streets away there was that French delicatessen. I dashed off there, bought orange juice, croissants—those chocolate ones you liked so much. On the way back, I bought a red rose . . . I was only gone about twenty minutes.' Jo clenched her hands in her lap, willing him to stop, but his voice went on remorselessly. 'When I got back, I arranged it all on my one and only tray, then took it in. The bed was rumpled, still warm—or so it seemed—from your body, but you weren't there. Then I found the note. I chased after you to Paddington—thought I might still be in time. I hung around there for hours before going to your hostel to check that, yes, you had left that morning. I must have only missed you by a few minutes.'

Their eyes met for a split second, then slid away quickly, as if unable to face the full implication of what he was saying. A few minutes, Jo thought, that's all it took, in the end, just a few minutes—to change my whole life, for ever.

'You do believe me, Jo, don't you?'

'Oh, yes, I believe you, Adam.' Jo's voice was unsteady for a moment. 'At least, over what happened that morning. But—you didn't love me, did you? Not really. I mean, if you had loved me, you would never have left it at that. You'd have followed me to Compton—or at least have written, if only to say it was all over. I would have understood—at least, I would have tried to. You decided that it was better for you—for your career—to end it, and I don't blame you for that now. But——' she drew a shuddering breath, feeling the oppression of that morning heavy on her spirits again, then went on, a hint of anger in her voice, '——not to write one line——'

'Jo!' Adam was staring at her, a stunned expression on his face. 'What the hell do you mean? Not write? I wrote—I telephoned that first day. The letters were never answered, and when I phoned your aunt said you'd gone straight on to stay with friends for a few days. You'd come home in a bit of a state—which I could well believe—but she would ask you if she should give me your address. I delayed going out to Rabbaq—I even came down here to see her——'

Jo put her hands to her ears and burst out wildly, 'No—it's not true! You're lying to me!'

'Whatever else I may have done to you,' he said sombrely, 'I've never lied to you. I came here, just before I left for Rabbaq, and she told me you'd gone to France, assuring her that you never wanted to see me again. She refused to give me your address—she said you'd forbidden it—and it never occurred to me to doubt her words.'

He stopped abruptly but Jo could not look at him, for she was locked into her own painful thoughts. Suddenly, everything fitted—her aunt's intense anxiety to see her safely away from Pear Trees . . . her almost palpable relief as she kissed Jo goodbye on the quayside . . . her smothering, cocooning care for Jo on her return from France . . . not one word of reproach, just shutting out entirely for her the world beyond their home—which Jo had been so grateful for at the time.

And then she saw again that day when Aunt Joan sat her down and told Jo her own story—of how she herself, no more than a girl, had been seduced then abandoned by a man. Abandoned also by her unforgiving parents, she had been forced to give up her baby daughter for adoption—and how Jo had been for her the child she had lost.

'. . . and men are all the same, my poor darling, You must know that now. But *I* shan't let you down. We'll see it through together, I promise you—just you and me against the world.' And Jo had put her head down on her aunt's shoulder and cried all the tears she had held back for so long . . .

'In any case, Jo, why didn't *you* try to contact me?'

Adam's voice was brusque but she didn't answer him at once. She was still grappling with this devastating transformation of the long-established images in her mind. It was as though Adam's words had shaken a child's kaleidoscope that she held in her hands. All the tiny pieces remained the same, but the pattern they formed was now very different.

'Why didn't you get in touch with me?' Adam repeated. 'Especially when you knew—when you realised you were pregnant?'

'I did—just once.' Jo spoke so quietly that he could hardly hear her words. 'For a long time I didn't. It was my pride, I suppose. I really did believe that you'd gone off without a word, that, as far as you were concerned, it was well and truly over . . . but then, finally, one day . . . when everything seemed even blacker than usual, I did write——'

'For God's sake, where did you send it to?' Adam demanded. 'I never got it.'

'Oh—I sent it to your old bedsitter, with "Please forward" on it—it was the only address I had, but it came back a couple of months later with "Not known" scrawled across it.'

'Well, what did you expect?' exclaimed Adam impatiently. 'Forwarding addresses don't last long in

Bedsitland. You should have contacted the University—or written to my home address.'

'I could have done.' Jo's voice was tired. 'But I think, subconsciously, I chose that address as the least likely to find you. As soon as I'd posted the letter I regretted sending it—and I was relieved, more than anything, when it came back. You see, I was so afraid of how you'd take it. No,' she went on as he tried to interrupt, 'you told me *I* had to choose—and I still don't think it was reasonable of you to face me with such an ultimatum—but *you* had a plain choice to make as well, Adam, and I thought you'd made it—that you'd decided to give me up, that your career mattered more to you. And anyway, it's easy for you to protest *now*, but putting me aside,' her voice became harsh, 'I certainly didn't think your well-laid plans would include being encumbered with a baby.'

Adam got up and went to stand by the mantelpiece. Without looking at her, he replied, 'You said just now that I never really knew you. I don't think you ever really knew me either.'

'Didn't I, Adam? Are you quite sure I didn't?'

Startled by the anger in her voice, he looked directly at her and she held his look. She smiled up at him, a bitter smile.

'Oh, it's all right for you to say that now—tonight; you've made it *now*. Your plans for Adam Roker have worked out just fine. You can afford to sit back and say that you'd have been glad to have Jon and me along—you may even convince yourself you mean it, and that you're a poor, hard-done-by deprived father—but just think back eight years. You were so single-minded, so determined to have things go your way—and what you've told me tonight only confirms that. No, Adam—I was afraid of your reaction. I thought you'd either demand that I have an abortion, which I wasn't prepared to do, or——' She stopped.

'Or?'

She hesitated, then went on rapidly, her face very pale, '—or that you might possibly think that you *had* to marry me, out of some sense of duty. And then you would feel that I'd trapped you, and grow to dislike—even hate me, and I couldn't have borne that.' Her voice quivered slightly, but she still managed to look up at him, and she saw that he was frowning.

'I've just thought of something else.' He came over and threw himself down on the sofa again. 'When I came down here that time—hoping against hope that you'd be here—your aunt said—at least, she hinted that you might be going to marry the son of the restaurateur in France. That would, no doubt, have been an ideal match from her point of view. What went wrong? I suppose you being pregnant put a stop to that little scheme.'

Jo stared at him ashen-faced as the full implication of what he was saying burst upon her exhausted brain. She wanted to believe he was lying in his teeth, but a cold inner voice told her otherwise. Still, she had to hide the depth of her shock and bewilderment from him and, trying desperately to keep her tone flippant, she said, 'That would have been rather difficult—Jean-Paul was a babe in arms at the time. I've heard of child marriages, but that would have been ridiculous.'

She choked on the words and he said brusquely, 'Don't cry, Jo. Please don't cry.'

'I'm not crying,' she said defiantly. 'I never cry,' then found that tears were pouring down her cheeks.

She dashed them away with her hand and got up precipitately, leaning her elbow on the high mantelpiece as she struggled for composure. Adam moved as though to come across to her, but she gestured him to remain where he was.

'I wasn't crying for myself,' she declared.

He gave a harsh laugh. 'Yes—it's no fun when your idol crashes to the ground, is it? Your dear aunt had feet of clay, it seems. And during all those months, I wonder if she ever, just once, wondered if she'd done the right thing. I very much doubt it.' He stood up with a violent movement and began to pace up and down the room. 'If I could get my hands on her——'

'No, don't say that.' Jo spoke quietly enough, but he was silenced. 'What she did to you—to us—was unforgivable, I know, but there *were* reasons—in her eyes, good reasons. And your hatred won't harm her now, but it will poison *your* life.'

'And *your* life, Jo—hasn't she poisoned that?'

'No—no, she hasn't.' She shook her head slowly. 'In fact, if I'm completely honest, the last eight years have done me a great deal of good. Yes, it's true,' she insisted, against his exclamation of protest. 'I was so unsure, so immature— surely you would agree with that?' There was a flash of steel in her voice. 'Now, I'm happy and fulfilled—my life is just the way I want it to be. True, it was bad at first, very bad, but it passed. Everything passes, you know, good and bad, in time. And now,' she paused, 'it's all behind me and——'

'Marry me, Jo.'

She gaped at him, her brain dull with fatigue. 'M- marry—what do you mean?'

'What I said. Marry me.'

She looked at him, stunned. 'Oh, no—no, Adam. Never—I shall never marry.'

'Never marry?' he repeated angrily. 'Why this sudden renunciation of the world in a girl of twenty-five? Are you planning on ending your days in a convent?'

'It's not sudden,' she retorted. 'I don't need marriage. I've got Pear Trees, and that's enough.'

'Enough! How can you say that a restaurant is enough for you?'

'But it is, Adam—and you must accept that!'

Jo banged her fists down on her knees in emphasis, but even as she spoke she knew that she was not telling the full truth. Her whole body shrank from the very thought of marriage and what it must inevitably entail. What could it mean to her but pain and unhappiness? The trauma of that dreadful night and the long months of desolation and heartbreak that followed it and with which it was inextricably intertwined were seared too deeply into her ever to be removed. She knew, in her heart, that this was why she had reacted so violently to Adam's kiss on the Heath.

She would never admit this to Adam. She could barely admit it to herself—but it was true. For her, fulfilment must be found elsewhere. She knew the truth now; she understood Adam—forgave him, even—and she wished desperately that she could make it up to him for the great wrong he had suffered—but not in this way. She knew now that over the past years she had hidden her fears of a physical relationship behind a façade of brisk efficiency, and there had been no difficulty in keeping at a cool arm's length several would-be admirers, including, at one time, Mark Sinclair.

Adam, though, was a man not so easily dismissed. She could see that many women would think her a fool to pass up this chance but—and she acknowledged this with a twinge of painful regret—marriage was not for her. She could even feel gratitude to Adam, that he had forced her to recognise, accept the truth about herself, but her feelings were now so deeply ingrained that she knew they would never change. She had to reconstruct the protective wall she had so painfully built around herself over eight years, and no one must be allowed to break through it again.

'No, Adam,' she said, forcing herself to speak more calmly. 'I'm sorry, but I don't want—I don't need—that sort of relationship with you again, ever. And too much has happened, to both of us, since we were—together. I'm very grateful for your proposal—I really am—and I can see now that I've misjudged you very badly. I hope that one day you'll be able to forgive me. But it wouldn't be fair to you— whatever you may think, I *know* I could never make you happy. No, Adam——' as he tried to protest '—you must face up to the truth. You can't bring back yesterday. I told you when you first came back that my life was happy. Well, it's more than happy—we're secure and contented, Jon and I.'

'Yes—Jon. I was coming to him.'

'W-what do you mean?' She was suddenly apprehensive.

'Well—he's my son, isn't he? What are you going to do about that?'

Jo's eyes narrowed as she looked at his face, deliberately expressionless. So that was it—this was what he had been leading up to. She smiled grimly to herself—she had actually been fool enough to think his offer of marriage had been made in generosity of spirit, an attempt to make up to her—but she had been wrong. He just wanted to get his possessive hands on Jon. Well, that made it easier.

'How do you mean?' she asked, playing for time.

'Well, I would have thought that was obvious. I want to get to know him before it's too late.'

'But it *is* too late,' she snapped, 'eight years too late. I'm not prepared to put at risk all that I've worked to build up, just so that you can walk in and have easy access to my son—and he is *my* son, Adam. I don't deny that you're his father, but that just happens to be a biological fact, nothing more.'

He came across and knelt by her chair; he forced her to turn her head and look straight into his eyes.

'You must let me get to know him, Jo.' He spoke quietly. 'I won't tell him I'm his father, without your permission, I promise. But you've got to let me in on him, even on the fringe. He *is* my son.'

'So you keep saying.' Jo's voice was savage and she glared at him.

His lips tightened. 'Give in gracefully, Jo. I don't want to hurt you.'

'I don't feel very graceful.'

He sighed. 'Jon will grow up one day—you can't prevent that. And you can't bind him to you for ever with steel cords—the more you try, the more he'll break free in the end. Ask yourself this—what will you have left when he's gone, if you build your whole life on him?'

'Oh—I shall still have Pear Trees—or another restaurant, if your syndicate tips me out,' she said lightly.

He stood up abruptly. 'Pear Trees! For God's sake, Johanna, is that to be your whole life for the next fifty years—first Jon, then a restaurant? But that's up to you, I suppose. As for Jon, all I want is for you to agree to let me get to know him—take him out occasionally.'

'No—no, I won't! I'm not giving him to you.'

He sighed again. 'Look, Jo—I don't want you to *give* him to me.' His voice was still patient, reasonable, but she sensed the steel in it. 'But he *is* my son, and you're not going to deprive me of him any longer—or him of me.'

'Deprive him of you? He doesn't need you!' Her voice

rose. 'He's *not* deprived—he's got me, hasn't he? He doesn't need anyone else.'

'That's a matter of opinion,' he said bleakly, 'from what I've seen of him so far—particularly tonight. If pressed, I would say that his foolish, doting mother is busy turning him into someone who's heading straight for the psychiatrist's couch in a few years' time—or worse. I suppose, in the circumstances, it's inevitable that you can't give Jon all the attention he clearly so desperately needs. And when he does see you, you're so busy trying to compensate by pussy-footing round him that you're turning him into a little tyrant. Ask yourself this—what's he going to be like in ten, twenty years' time, and if the thought doesn't appal you, it ought to. But I warn you, Johanna, I'm not going to stand by and watch it. I'll fight you if I have to—and I'll win, because I'm right and in your heart of hearts you know I am.'

Jo was breathing so fast, she felt suffocated. She leapt up, pushing him aside, snatched up his jacket, which he had thrown on a chair, and flung it at him, her eyes green with passion.

'Get out—get out of here!' she raged, and without another word he went.

CHAPTER SEVEN

THE last conscious thing Jo did, as she crawled wearily into bed, was to set her alarm clock, but when its shrill screech sounded, she was already awake. When she looked in on Jon he was still lost in the drugged sleep of exhaustion, so she decided to let him sleep on and after she had showered and forced down some toast and coffee she rang the school to say she would bring him in at lunch-time. Then she poured herself another cup of coffee and retreated to the sitting-room with it.

As she sat down, there was Jon's book, still on the coffee-table where she had put it down with shaking hands a few hours previously. Hopelessly, she flicked open the cover and saw again the damning evidence. She just might, she reflected, have been able to persuade Adam that he was not Jon's father—that she had been double-timing him with someone else—although that would have been difficult enough, but the name convicted her. Jo had insisted on that one concession, in the face of Aunt Joan's tight-lipped disapproval—even in the depths of her desolation she had retained the bitter-sweet memory of Adam's love.

Jo's mouth twisted suddenly. Aunt Joan—what inward battles her aunt must have fought to convince herself that she was right, ruthlessly to prise her beloved niece from the grip of Adam Roker. Adam—for eight years Jo had hugged to herself the thought of his careless seduction, his casual abandonment. But the bitterness, the anger, were now replaced by feelings of regret and guilt. He too had been the victim of deception and betrayal. Jo faced squarely the thought of how Adam must have suffered—in his way, at least as much as she. And she had loved him so much that even now, with that love long dead, she felt a violent stab of pain at the thought.

Her mind moved to the dreadful scene they had walked in on last night—she felt a burning humiliation at the memory of Jon and at how utterly helpless she had been. She was forced to acknowledge that Adam was right. She couldn't any longer shut her eyes to the truth—Jon was rapidly becoming uncontrollable and desperately needed a firmer hand than she could bring herself to use. Then Adam's words came back to her ... Supposing, in later years, Jon learned the truth, that she had deprived him of his father—not for his own sake, but for her own selfish reasons—might he not turn against her ... Jo felt sick with fear at the picture she was building up.

Adam had even offered to marry her for Jon's sake. If he was prepared to do this surely she must make some sacrifice, too. She must be prepared to allow Adam and Jon to see each other sometimes—to become friends. It was only right and fair, for both their sakes. Not quite yet, perhaps, but soon ... This would inevitably mean that she too would see more of Adam. How, she asked herself, did she feel about that? Who knows? It might even, in time, be possible for them to build up some sort of friendship, albeit an uneasy one. Unless, of course, he were to marry the woman in the photograph. That, at least, would solve everything. Anyway, she was sure that somehow she would cope.

She heard nothing of Adam over the next few days. From Bobbie and Daphne she received regular bulletins: landscape architects were carrying out a preliminary survey of the estate ... renovation work was starting on the manor ... the lake was being dredged ... a van load of porpoises was on its way . . . Jo treated the wilder rumours with disdain and did her best to ignore the others totally.

As usual, the following Saturday morning, Jo took Jon into Broadston; it was their weekly outing together, which they both looked forward to. She left him in the sweet shop, choosing his weekly ration, and went round to the dry cleaner's to collect a couple of items, then they walked back together to the square, where she had parked the car. They always ended up in the little café nearby for a drink. There was no hurry to get back—Saturday evenings were busy but lunchtimes were very slack. Most people seemed to prefer to do their shopping, then rush off home to their gardens or an afternoon's sport on the television. Aunt Joan had been toying with the idea of dropping Saturday lunches altogether but Jo was reluctant to do that, and as they walked, she was considering—perhaps a cold buffet table, lots of salads—Bobbie happily spent hours concocting salads . . .

'Oh, look, Mummy, there's Adam. He's seen us—he's waving.'

Before Jo could stop him, Jon had wriggled free from her restraining hand and had darted off towards him. Jo leaned against the car with her arms folded, feeling slightly sick. Caught unawares, all her good intentions evaporated instantly as she watched the meeting between the two and when Adam looked in her direction she ignored him, deliberately turning her back and getting into the car. Surely, she thought, he'll take the hint, but a few minutes later, when she glanced in the driving-mirror, she saw them both walking towards her, in lively conversation. Very slowly, she got out, meeting Adam's half-smile with a freezing look.

Jon's face was radiant with excitement. 'Mummy—

Adam's going fishing tomorrow, on a boat—right out to sea.'

'How nice, Jon.' She glanced at her watch ostentatiously. 'We must be going now,' and she put her hand on the door handle.

'But, *Mummy*—Adam says I can go with him. That's if you'll let me, of course,' he added carefully.

'Go with him?' she repeated. 'No—of course you can't go with him, Jon.'

She looked down at her son, seeing his face cloud, and added in a softer tone. 'No—I'm sorry, Jon, but it's out of the question. You know you're not over your cough—and, besides, you've only just got your ten-metre swimming badge from school.'

'Oh, that's all right, Mummy. Adam says there's a life jacket that'll fit me on the boat—and oilskins, just like his yellow ones he's got in the——'

Jo's eyes went over her son's head to Adam, standing with his hand on the boy's shoulder, and she favoured him with one searing look before turning back to Jon. 'No, I'm sorry, Jon, but I'd rather you didn't.'

She was half afraid that he would throw a tantrum there and then, but to her amazement he only bit his lip. 'All right, Mummy.' He tried to smile up at her. 'I 'spect I'd have been seasick anyway—I've never been in a boat.' His mouth quivered and he opened the car door. ''Bye, Adam.'

All at once, he looked what he was—a very small, thin, defenceless little boy—and the old knife turned in Jo's heart. She stood still for a moment, oblivious of the shoppers milling around on the pavement, then, trying to speak nonchalantly but not looking at him, she said to Adam, 'You'd take good care of him?'

'Of course,' he said seriously. 'But just in case you're still wondering, yes—I'd take very great care of—*your* son, Jo.'

She opened the rear door and smiled rather tremulously in at Jon, who had buried himself in the far corner of the seat behind a comic. 'It's all right, love. I was just being a bit silly—you can go if you really want to.'

When Jon, his face dazzling once more, had finished hugging her, Adam took out his wallet and extracted a note. 'Do something for me, will you, Jon? I'd like you to go and get some bars of chocolate for us to take tomorrow— good, solid ones, mind. I don't want you getting hungry.'

They both followed him with their eyes as he darted off towards the sweet shop, then Jo said, 'Well, I suppose you're satisfied now.' Her voice was very cold—the pleasure of seeing Jon's face alight once more with joy had been very transitory.

'What do you mean?'

'Oh, come off it, Adam—you know exactly what I mean. It's what you've intended all along.'

'Jo—I swear it wasn't. My waterproofs and sea-boots were all over the back seat of the car, and Jon was interested.'

'Yes—so, of course, you just happened to mention that, surprise, surprise, you were going on a trip tomorrow.'

'Well—not exactly. He was so keen, it just sort of happened. All right—maybe I should have asked you first, but——'

'But you knew what I'd say,' she said flatly, thinking angrily, this isn't how I've planned it—I know I'd intended that Jon *should* meet Adam but not so soon, not so fast . . .

'For goodness sake, Jo!' He frowned with impatience. 'This isn't some cunning, devious plot to winkle all Jon's affections away from you. I just want to give him a good day out—and I'll make sure he has just that.'

When Jon had handed over a paper bag full of chocolate

bars, and Adam's change, he said to his mother, 'Don't let's bother with a drink, Mummy—I want to go home and start getting ready,' and he climbed back into the car.

'Right,' said Adam, 'well, I'll see you tomorrow. Max keeps his boat down near Lyme, so I'll collect Jon just after six.'

Jo, looking at him, saw—or at any rate fancied she saw— a gleam of jubilation, even triumph, in his eyes and her frustration boiled over.

'Oh, shut up. Just shut up,' she said, her voice low but vicious. 'You've won, haven't you? Just go and enjoy your victory somewhere else.'

The fishing trip was a great success, at least to judge from Jon's never-ending chatter the following day, and looking at his flushed, bright face, Jo reluctantly accepted that she had been right to give in. Even so, she had felt nothing but relief when Adam, dropping Jon off, had mentioned that he was going abroad on business and would be away for some time. He had glanced at her as he spoke but she had merely smiled coolly and said, 'Have fun—or whatever it is you jet-setting businessmen have,' and so, with a last goodbye to Jon, he had left.

She tried to forget him in her work, and might have managed it if Jon had not talked about 'Adam' incessantly until she felt like screaming. Also, a steady stream of postcards from exotic places arrived for Jon, which he insisted on showing off proudly to her admiring staff, before pinning them up on his bedroom wall, so that she was conscious of them—and the sender—every time she went into his room. Still, she reflected grimly, Adam at arm's length—or rather, postcard distance—she could cope with. It was the man himself—intimidating, even threatening—whom she lived in trepidation of seeing.

Then Jon became ill and was off school for three weeks, so that Adam slipped uneasily to the back of her mind, lost in a welter of running Pear Trees, caring for Jon—and stifling her feelings of guilt. Every winter, Jon had bad colds which invariably ended on his chest, and the previous winter had been no exception. But the hacking cough had virtually cleared up when one of his school-friends had invited him to go swimming at the local outdoor pool. The weather, even by the standards of an average English June, had been chill and grey, but Jo, seizing the chance of a quiet Saturday afternoon to prepare for a dinner party in the restaurant that evening, had overcome her doubts and given in. In a matter of days Jon developed bronchitis, then a touch of bronchial pneumonia, Doctor Grey made daily visits and Jo, tense and exhausted, had nursed him through several worrying days.

One afternoon in early July, when Jon was at last back at school, Jo was sitting at the kitchen table in Pigsties, carefully writing out menu cards when, behind her, the door burst open, her hand jerked, and the pen skidded across the cream card. Throwing it down with an angry exclamation, she swung round, to see—Adam, framed in the doorway. Her heart leapt against her ribs, but she managed to turn her start of pure terror into a movement to snatch up her pen and she eyed him coldly.

'I thought you were still away—in Hong Kong, or wherever.'

He pulled out a chair, sat down opposite her, and said abruptly, 'I've just seen Bobbie in the village. She tells me Jon's been ill.'

Jo's lips tightened and two warning spots of colour appeared on her cheekbones. Well, thank you very much Bobbie, she thought.

'Why didn't you tell me?' His voice was accusing. 'Why did you leave it to someone else to let me know our—*my* son was ill?'

She gathered the sprawl of menu cards together with a controlled movement before, icy-faced, she allowed herself to look at him.

'That would have been rather difficult, considering you were on the other side of the world—and, as far as I'm aware, hadn't left me a forwarding address,' she added with heavy sarcasm.

His brows came down in the familiar scowl. 'Oh, come off it, Jo. You know very well you could have got hold of me if you'd wanted to—but of course you didn't.'

She ignored this gibe and contented herself with retorting, 'And anyway, what business is it of yours?' but then, at the look in his eyes, her own fell.

She pushed back her chair and stood up precipitately. 'I was just going to make a cup of tea—d'you want one?'

While he sat, his arms folded on the table, she clattered around, the actions giving her a much-needed vent for her feelings. Finally, she banged down the tea things on the table and sat down again.

'Oh, and by the way, next time you feel you *have* to come here, do please feel free to use the front door, like other *outsiders*. Not even my staff burst in through my kitchen door unless it's some dire emergency.'

He ran his fingers through his hair, then said, in a softer tone, 'Look, Jo, you know how twittery new fathers are supposed to be! So you must make allowances for me.'

He gave her a disarming grin which got under her guard for a moment, giving her a tight feeling in her throat. While she was still slightly off balance, Adam reached across the table and took her hand, holding it firmly so that she could not withdraw it. He looked down at her palm and gave an exclamation.

'You've burned yourself!'

She shrugged. 'Occupational hazard. I did it lifting a meat-dish out of the oven a couple of weeks back—I suppose I was rushing. It was rather nasty, but it's perfectly all right now,' she added firmly, but even as she spoke he bent his head and gently put his lips to the tender spot. Jo jerked her hand back as though she had just been burned again and, to cover her confusion, hastily poured a cup of tea and thrust the plate of biscuits across to Adam's side of the table, her skin tingling all the while with the sensation of his warm lips.

At last, she looked at him across the rim of her teacup. 'Anyway, please don't worry about Jon. He's fine now. True, he wasn't very well—in fact,' honesty compelled her to admit, 'he *was* quite ill for a few days. But he's a lot better now, just a bit run down.' Her voice had softened a little. After all, it was understandable that Adam had been concerned. 'Doctor Grey's very pleased with him—he let him go back to school on Monday. He says a change of air would do Jon good, so I'm hoping to take him to the seaside for a few days in August.'

Adam replaced his cup with extreme care and looked up at her. He drew a deep breath, then said, 'Even before I met Bobbie, I was coming to see you today, Jo. I'm going back to Rabbaq next week—and I'm taking Jon.'

CHAPTER EIGHT

STUNNED, Jo could only sit staring at Adam across the table, unable quite to comprehend the enormity of what he had said. Finally, she stammered, 'Rabbaq? Take Jon to Rabbaq? What on earth do you mean?'

'What I say. I'm going back out there for a couple of weeks, and he can come with me.' As she still gaped at him, he went on rapidly, 'If you must know, I wasn't too happy with him on the fishing trip—I'm not really surprised that he's been ill. He looked very pale and thin compared with Max's two boys—and he was coughing quite badly then.'

He glanced across at her, as though to gauge her reaction, but Jo's expression was blank and he continued firmly, 'So this will give him the change of air he needs. I'm sure there won't be any trouble getting him off school so near the end of term but if there is, I'll give the Head a ring, explain the situation.'

Jo, listening to his smoothly confident words, almost leapt across the table at him, punching and kicking, but she restrained this impulse. He would only hold her at arm's length until she calmed down or, worse still, gather her tightly into his arms so she couldn't struggle, as he had done with Jon on that frightful night.

At last, hardly trusting herself to speak, she swallowed then said, her voice dangerously quiet, 'There'll be no trouble, because he isn't going. He is *not* going.'

Completely disregarding her, Adam went on, 'I've got some good friends out there, with a boy of Jon's age. He'll

110

have a marvellous time.'

Jo's eyes dilated with terror as it finally sank in. Jon—go abroad with Adam, have his undivided attention for two whole weeks? Suddenly, the dark, unspoken—barely acknowledged—fear that had lurked in her mind ever since Adam had returned, leaped out at her. How could she possibly hope to compete with him in any battle for their son's affections? A day's fishing-trip had been bad enough, but this was something altogether different—so exciting, so glamorous, compared with anything she could provide. Her 'few days at the seaside'—they just weren't in the same league! No, whatever happened, Jon must not be allowed to go with Adam. She knew better than anyone how fatally easy it was to fall under his spell. Jon would inevitably grow close to him and that was something she simply could not endure.

When she spoke, though, her voice was controlled. 'I'm sorry, Adam, but I have to say no. He—he's already had enough time off school——'

'But it's almost the end of term. He'll hardly miss a thing, I'm sure.'

'——and anyway, it would unsettle him too much.'

'Nonsense—he'd just have the time of his young life. We'd all see to that.'

'We'! Was this some sort of conspiracy, dreamed up by Adam and these friends of his, to win Jon over to his side? Surely not—and yet Jo knew only too well how ruthlessly single-minded, how careless of the cost, Adam could be when he set his sights on achieving an objective.

She had been picking compulsively at the lace trim on her handkerchief, but now she looked up, stony-faced, and, seeing her expression, Adam's eyes hardened. 'I'm taking him, Jo, and that's an end of it.'

His voice was still smooth, but there was a warning hint of menace beneath the surface which put her hackles up still further. He might terrify the wits out of his business opponents but he's *not* going to frighten me, she thought grimly. But even so, there was a faint tremor in her voice. 'You're not taking him. I won't allow it, and I'll—I'll take you to court to stop you, if necessary.'

Adam laughed. 'Don't be so absurd, Jo. You'd be wasting your time—and money—and if you don't believe me, ask your precious Sinclair. Take me to court! And just what effect do you think that would have on Jon? I'm not asking for custody, for God's sake. I'm not snatching him from you for ever in some awful tug of love, but I do have some rights. However much you may hate the fact, I *am* his father.'

He broke off abruptly and leaned back in his chair, watching her, as if coolly assessing her reaction. But Jo's mouth was set in a mutinous line and she looked at him with real loathing, as he went on, 'You admit yourself Jon needs a change of air—well, the dry warmth out there will be the perfect tonic for him. By the way, how exactly did Jon get this latest cold? Bobbie was babbling something about an outdoor swimming-pool.'

Damn Bobbie, Jo thought savagely. And damn Adam— he had obviously found out all about it and was quite unashamedly using the guilt he must know she was feeling to pressurise her still further. And yet, in the midst of her anger, she knew he was right. It *was* exactly what Jon needed before the next winter set in, all too soon.

He was still watching her. 'Don't worry, Jo, I'll bring him back safely. After all, I returned him from the fishing-trip in one piece, didn't I?'

'Yes, but that was only a few hours,' Jo retorted, but even as she spoke the image returned to her of Jon's bubbling excitement over that one day. She couldn't wait, she thought sourly, to see his face at the prospect of a whole glorious fortnight with Adam.

'It would be a chance in a million for him, believe me. And I'll admit—I *want* to take him. I'll enjoy it too. I've told you before—he's one of the nicest kids around.'

Jo regarded her adversary coldly. 'You sound as though you've had a great deal of experience of the breed—children, I mean.'

'After spending half my working-life trying to get the better of hard-headed wheeler-dealers, kids are a refreshing change—at least, the ones I know are.'

Without warning, something that had niggled on for weeks at the back of Jo's consciousness burst like a bubble in her mind and before she could stop herself, she had blurted out, 'And they're the ones in the photo, I suppose?'

He frowned in genuine puzzlement. 'What photo?'

Too late, Jo realised the trap she had laid for herself and leaped into with both feet. She felt hot all over at the thought of having to admit that she had been snooping in Adam's bedroom.

'Oh—nothing. Forget it,' she said hastily.

'No—I'm intrigued. What photo? Unless——' his eyes glinted and seemed to bore into her '——Jo, do you mean the one in my flat?'

She swallowed. 'Yes. I—I went into your room—just for a moment—and saw it.' Even to her own ears, her voice was feeble and, angry at being forced on to the defensive, she attacked. 'You're going on about Jon—why don't you take them, and their mother? I presume she's a "good friend" of yours. You'll have all the children you want if——'

'Jo, for heaven's sake.' To her astonishment, he was actually laughing. 'That's Carol.'

'Carol?'

'Yes—my sister. She and her family are into organic farming in a big way. They live half-way up a mountain in deepest Wales and she's very happy, but once in a while she gets the bug.'

'The bug?'

'Yes—you know, the irresistible urge to feel the city pavements under her feet and snuff the sweet smell of exhaust fumes instead of the manure heap. Rod—her husband—is very understanding. He drives her to the station and she bolts off up to me for a few days—she even keeps her city clothes at my flat.'

'Yes, I know. I—I mean——'

'How do you know?' Then, when she didn't answer, he went on, the hint of a smile lurking round his lips, 'Oh, I see. You had a really good look round, didn't you? If you'd only asked, I'd have given you a guided tour. You know, Jo,' his voice was reflective, 'if I didn't know you better, I'd think that you were keeping tabs on me!'

She opened her mouth to make a cutting retort but shut it again, biting her lower lip. There was no way round it. She *was* in the wrong—and not simply in prying in his flat. That was a minor detail. No—yet again she had misjudged him, thinking the worst of him. What a fool she'd made of herself, what a fool!

As though sensing her inner turmoil, Adam pressed home his advantage. 'Well, now that we've cleared up that little misunderstanding, let's get back to Jon. I take it you've got no more objections. Surely you won't try to stop me, knowing it will do him so much good?'

Jo finished shredding her handkerchief. She was beginning to feel like a hunted rabbit which, no matter how it twists and turns, still feels the stoat's hot breath on its back. Adam had cut the ground from under her feet. He was right, of course—it *would* do Jon good, and she knew she couldn't live with the guilt of denying him a once-in-a-lifetime holiday—although how she would get through those two weeks, not knowing but guessing only too well the hold that Adam would inexorably be gaining on his affections . . .

'Of course——' He paused.

'Yes?'

'I was just going to say——' He paused again, this time for so long that she looked up.

'Well?'

'I was thinking,' his voice was very matter of fact, 'if you're so worried about me exerting a nefarious influence over Jon——' She started at his words, for it was as though he had reached into her mind and unerringly exposed the hidden fears that lay there '——you could always come as well.'

She gaped at him. Her mind, normally so agile, was totally unable to grapple with yet another wholly unexpected twist. At last she spoke. 'No—that's impossible.' She hunted feverishly for a plausible excuse. 'I—I couldn't possibly leave Pear Trees, you must know that.'

'Oh, that's no problem. July-August is your slack time—people away and so on. I've checked with Bobbie, and she says they can easily cope without you for a couple of weeks.'

'You've checked with Bobbie!' Jo reddened with anger. 'Once and for all, keep away from my staff—and stop organising my life for me behind my back!'

Adam raised his hands in mock apology. 'OK—OK! But it doesn't alter the facts—you *could* get away, if you want to. Anyway, that's it. I'm taking Jon—even if it means his mother tagging along too!'

All at once, Jo was quite unable to battle with him any longer.

'All right, Adam. Jon can go with you.'

'And you?'

'Yes.' Her voice was drained of emotion. 'Yes—I'll come too.'

CHAPTER NINE

As the aircraft doors were opened, a stifling blanket of heat rolled into the plane, and outside, although it was late afternoon, the tarmac shimmered under a burning haze, so that it was bliss to reach the air-conditioned coolness of the airport reception area. To Jon and Jo everything was glamour and strangeness although, in truth, Dhabra Airport had the bland anonymity of airports the world over. Adam dealt quickly and efficiently with the Customs formalities—Jo was staggered to hear him talking Arabic with fluent ease although she refused to be impressed, reminding herself that, after all, he had lived in Rabbaq for several years.

As they emerged into the heat again, a dark-skinned Arab in white robes stepped forward, saluted Adam and gestured them towards a grey limousine. Jo was still coming to terms with this VIP reception as the car nosed its way through the narrow city streets. Jon sat silent, his eyes like huge saucers, and she too felt quite overwhelmed by the kaleidoscope of impressions; gleaming skyscrapers cheek by jowl with shadowy open-fronted shops ... enormous American cars jostling for position with ox-carts ... car horns blaring above raucous, unfamiliar music ... exotic smells of spices and frying food ... pavement cafés, just two or three tables, with leathery-faced old men playing backgammon ... people, people everywhere—or rather, she corrected herself, men, for there were very few women or girls to be seen.

117

The early twilight was settling as they left the suburbs and began to climb up into low hills, dotted with scrub and rocky outcrops. As every mile brought her nearer to their destination, Jo fought to quell the butterflies of apprehension—almost panic—that were fluttering around inside her. The questions, fears, which had lurked uneasily in her mind ever since, in her folly, she had agreed to come could not now be thrust away. What had Adam told his friends? How much did they know about the past—Jo swallowed—about Jon? As his close friends, they might well be hostile towards her. If he *had* told them about Jon, they would no doubt only have heard his version—that she had deprived Adam of his son for seven years. Over Jon's head, she stole a look at him, but he was leaning back in the soft upholstery, obviously quite at ease.

She cleared her throat and he looked at her quizzically. 'Er—your friends . . . do they,' she picked her words with extreme care, conscious of the child between them, 'do they know *all* about us?'

Adam would surely pick up the hidden significance of her question, but he merely replied, 'Oh, yes, Ali and Stella know everything they need to know.'

His dark eyes glinted with secret, malicious amusement and Jo flushed with anger. He was tantalising her, trading on the insecurity she was bound to be feeling, and she turned her head away as the car swung off the road, between two tall white pillars and up a narrow winding track. A few minutes later, they rounded a bend and Jo saw a sprawling collection of low white buildings scattered around central gardens, which were laid out with palm trees and flowering shrubs.

'Ah, we've arrived,' Adam said.

'Your friends live here?' Jo gasped, trying to keep the

same awe out of her voice as was evident on Jon's face.

'Yes—at least, this is their summer house. They have another one down on the plain.'

Jo felt a sinking sensation in the pit of her stomach as she looked out at the immaculate grounds. Adam had told her next to nothing about his friends—Ali, he had said, was a fellow petroleum engineer—and Jo had not thought to ask. She had expected a flat, or at most a house in some suburb of the town—but this! Dry-mouthed, she stared out of the car window.

'Mummy, look—a swimming-pool!'

It was the first time that Jon had spoken since they had left the airport and following his excited gaze Jo saw in the half-light the glimmer of blue water, almost hidden among the trees.

'That's right, Jon,' said Adam. 'You'll be able to swim there tomorrow.'

The car drew up outside a low white bungalow, separated from the rest of the complex by a white latticed stone wall and surrounded by more gardens. Almost before it had stopped, two menservants came down the steps from the veranda and whisked away their luggage. The interior of the bungalow, although not air-conditioned, was deliciously cool. A young maidservant came forward and bowed shyly to Jo.

'This is Jasmin,' said Adam, smiling at the girl, who gave him a radiant smile in return. 'She'll take you and Jon to your suite—my rooms are down here.' He gestured towards a passage which ran obliquely down the bungalow. 'And that's another of your little worries settled!'

Jo felt herself going pink under the sardonic mockery of his expression. But he was right, of course. For days, another question had racked her mind: if, as she had now

convinced herself, Adam's friends *did* know about the past,
wouldn't they have naturally assumed—perhaps with some
little help from Adam—that they would be sharing a
bedroom—even a bed? Although clearly aware of her
thoughts, Adam went on casually, 'Jasmin will unpack for
you later. Have a shower and recover a bit—you both look
whacked—and then Stella's asked us to join them for
dinner.'

She and Jon followed the girl down a tiled corridor to
their rooms. Hers was large and high, with an old-fashioned
ceiling-fan which made a pleasant downward draught. It
had the same cool tiled floor and was simply, almost
sparsely, furnished, with dark carved furniture and bright
woven rugs. Through an open door she glimpsed a small
bathroom. Jon's room, just across the passage, was much
smaller, although he had his own tiny shower area. The
walls were decorated with colourful posters, there was a
pile of toys and jigsaws by the bed and the bed itself—
unlike Jo's, which had cool coverings with very much an
Eastern feel to them—had an English-type pillow case and
duvet cover, with a brilliant pattern of toy soldiers. A lot of
thought had gone into making the room cheerful and
comforting—if Jon should need a little comfort—and Jo's
heart warmed gratefully.

She left Jon to shower and lie down on his bed, then
returned to her own room. The sweat from the overpower-
ing heat at the airport had dried on her skin, leaving her
feeling tacky and dusty, and she enjoyed a long, cool
shower. She decided there was not time to wash and dry her
hair and she was just recombing it back into place when
there was a knock at the door and, in the mirror, she saw
Adam come in. She dropped her comb and hastily drew the
neck of her cotton housecoat together, conscious that it had

fallen open to reveal the swell of her breasts. But Adam didn't seem to notice.

'Sorry to burst in on you, but I suddenly remembered something. What are you going to wear to dinner?'

'Well—that blouse and skirt.'

Jo gestured reluctantly towards the bed, where she had laid out a dark print cotton skirt and an equally simple white blouse. Before leaving, Adam had offered to buy her and Jon as many new clothes for the trip as she wanted. Her pride stung, she had rejected his offer, but now that they had arrived, and she had seen exactly where they would be staying, she wished she had given just a little more thought to her wardrobe. Still, Jon would be fine and that was something—shorts, T-shirts and jeans were children's holiday uniform the world over. She watched, faintly resentful, as he picked up the blouse and looked at it critically.

'What's the matter—afraid I'll disgrace you in front of your friends?'

He turned, still holding the blouse, and gave her a long, considering look. Then he dropped the blouse on the bed, came over and put his hands lightly on her shoulders. She could feel his body very close to hers and began pleating the skirt of her housecoat, unwilling to look up and meet his eyes in the glass.

'Relax, Jo. They'll like you—and you'll like them, if you let yourself. Please do like them—they're my very good friends. And don't worry.'

'I'm not worried,' she snapped. 'Why should I be? I was just thinking.' Her lips twisted wryly. 'It's rather amusing, I suppose. Years ago, you weren't considered good enough for me—now, well, the tables are turned with a vengeance, aren't they? You having to come and give my clothes the once-over, to make sure they're up to the required standard.'

His grip tightened on her shoulders momentarily and he shook her. 'Jo, don't be a fool. You don't have to prove to me how super-tough you are. And as for your clothes, I wasn't giving them the once-over, as you call it—or at least, only that I wanted you to be relaxed at dinner because you were wearing the right things. Ali's very European in his outlook and family life, but this is a very conservative country and when the servants are around you must please, for their sake, be well covered. I'm sure Ali wouldn't mind, himself, if you wore a low-cut, sleeveless dress, but you mustn't. This,' he gestured towards the bed, 'will be fine— long sleeves and buttoned up to the neck. Come to think about it, I suppose I was rather foolish to think you might be considering wearing anything else.'

She looked up hotly, but he had dropped his hands and was walking towards the door. He turned back for a moment.

'Oh, and by the way—there's no law here which says you have to pin your hair up in a cast-iron bun. You'd be surprised how much prettier you'd look with it down on your shoulders.'

'It isn't a bun.'

She glared at him in the mirror but he only laughed and retreated, saying, 'I'll go and see if Jon's ready.'

She had finished defiantly putting her hair up when he returned. 'Jon says he's too tired to get up, so I've asked Jasmin to look after him—she'll bring him supper on a tray.'

'But she can't look after him—she's far too young,' Jo objected, but Adam smiled.

'She may be young, but she's already got two children of

her own. They marry young here—they believe it keeps the youngsters out of trouble, and I'm not sure they're not right.' He glanced at her. 'And you needn't feel sorry for her—Jasmin's a very contented young lady. Her husband is one of the gardeners here, and they have their own little house in the grounds. So don't worry about Jon—his only problem is she'll spoil him even worse than you do, especially because he's a boy.'

Jo picked up her bag in silence and went across to Jon's room. She had wanted him with her, to provide a small but solid bulwark between her and Adam, but he was sitting up in bed, reading a book, a large iced orange drink at his elbow, and he kissed her goodnight with every appearance of contentment, so she had no option but to leave him to it.

Outside, night had come and Jo temporarily forgot her nervousness as they walked through the gardens under the dark sapphire sky. Sweet scents came from the flowering shrubs and overhead the stiff branches of the palms rustled mysteriously, while after the stifling heat of the day, the night air felt cool and tingling against her skin. The bungalow Adam made for was larger than the rest, with a wide veranda running the length of one side. A man and woman, sitting in cushioned basket chairs, got up and came towards them as they mounted the steps.

Adam's hand rested lightly on the back of her waist, propelling her forward. 'Jo, I'd like you to meet two very old friends of mine—Ali and Stella.'

The man, shorter and slighter than Adam, took her hand. 'My dear Miss Thornton, I am so glad to meet you at last.'

Jo murmured a polite reply, thinking, at last? How long had they known about her? Just how much had Adam told them? She shot him a searching glance, but his smile was bland.

The woman was smiling warmly at her. 'It's so nice to have you with us, Jo—I hope you'll let us call you that.'

Jo, usually cool and reserved with strangers, found herself smiling back at her. Stella was petite and plump and, though not pretty, her face had an irresistibly cheerful, open look. She drew Jo down on to a cane chaise-longue saying, 'We'll eat soon—you must be hungry, but I'm sure you'd like a cold fruit juice first.'

A servant appeared with a tray and poured drinks from a frosty glass jug. Jo sipped hers tentatively, then exclaimed, 'It's lovely—really delicious!'

Stella smiled. 'I'm glad you like it. It's my own invention—pineapple, orange, grape juice, with a dash of lime—everything picked fresh from our own garden.' She sipped her own drink then went on, 'We're having quite a simple meal—I thought that after the flight you wouldn't want anything too exotic.'

'But perhaps,' put in Ali, 'we can put on a *mansaf* for Jo some time while she's here.'

They laughed and Jo looked questioning.

'A special Bedouin feast,' Adam explained, 'for honoured guests—a whole sheep, a whole baby camel, a whole goat—and that's just the hors d'oeuvres!'

Jo smiled uncertainly, not sure how to take his words, and turned to Stella. 'Thank you for making Jon's room so welcoming—it was you, wasn't it?'

'Well, yes—at least, the children helped me. And talking of children,' she turned to Adam, 'they were desperate to come to the airport to meet Uncle Adam, but in the end I promised them they could all come and see you after dinner for a little while.' She saw Jo's face and smiled. 'Don't worry,

Jo—they sometimes seem like a marauding army but there are actually only five of them. Although,' she smiled across at her husband, 'we wanted you to be among the first to know, Adam—I'm expecting another child.'

Adam took her hand between his and kissed it. 'I'm so glad, Stella—congratulations.'

'Yes—Stella is aiming for a complete baseball team,' Ali remarked to Jo, so gravely that until she saw his eyes twinkling she hardly realised he was joking. He has a good face, she thought—thin and intelligent, with brilliant eyes that seem to penetrate your closest thoughts.

She watched the three of them chatting easily together and, although they were punctilious in drawing her into the conversation, none the less she felt herself slightly an intruder and had a twinge of sadness—if things had turned out differently, Ali and Stella would have been *her* friends too. She envied them their relaxed camaraderie—leading such a closed existence for so long, she had never had time, or inclination, to make intimate friends. In fact, she supposed that now Aunt Joan was dead, Bobbie was really the only person she allowed to get close to her, to have the occasional glimpse of the real Johanna Thornton.

Later, over their meal of lamb kebabs served on a bed of watercress, she talked about the flight and how much Jon had enjoyed it—and she herself. 'It was quite an experience. I've never flown before—in fact, I've never been abroad before, except years ago to France.' She broke off suddenly, her face hot, and glanced at Adam but he seemed quite unaware of what she had said. Hastily changing the subject, she turned to Stella, 'But you're not from Rabbaq, surely?'

'No—no, I'm Canadian by birth, although I've lived here since we married, of course.'

They went back to the veranda and several servants

appeared noiselessly, bringing coffee and tea.

'And what do you think of our servants?' Ali was smiling wickedly at her. 'I saw you casting your professional eye over them—I hope they measure up to the standard of your waiters?'

'Oh, good heavens,' Stella laughed, 'I'd clean forgotten what an expert you are, Jo. Adam's told us all about the party he went to at your restaurant. I daren't tell our cook, in case it frightens him.'

'Oh, I enjoyed the meal very much,' Jo murmured, but her mind was in a whirl. So Adam had told them about the Sandersons' party—she was beginning to wonder if there was anything—*anything*—he hadn't told them about her.

As she toyed with her coffee-spoon uncomfortably, there was a pattering of bare feet and a group of children burst out of a doorway with shrieks of joy—four boys, the oldest about Jon's age, and one little girl, the image of Stella, about two years old. Adam swept her up into his arms to save her from being trampled underfoot by her brothers, who tumbled all over him until he almost disappeared under a sea of brown limbs and bodies.

Ali plucked them off firmly one by one. 'Children, you are forgetting yourselves—come and meet our guest.'

To Jo's amazement, they immediately lined up in front of her and, feeling rather like Maria confronted with the young von Trapps, she shook hands gravely with each of them. The oldest boy, a miniature of his father, said, 'I do hope you will enjoy your holiday with us, Miss Thornton.'

Duty done, they turned their attention back to Adam and tried to drag him to his feet. 'Come and swim, Uncle Adam, come and swim.'

All at once, Jo felt exhausted. She stood up abruptly. 'I— I hope you won't all think I'm very rude if I leave you now.

It's been a long day, and I'm rather tired.'

Then, as Adam tried to disentangle himself, she smiled a goodnight which included them all and walked quickly down the veranda steps and into the shadowy garden. Once out of earshot, she slowed her hurrying steps and when she came to a small circular pool with fountains playing softly she sat down on the low parapet, trailing her fingers in the water. She sat there for quite a long time until she thought she heard distant voices, Adam's among them. Almost guiltily, she got to her feet and hurried on to the bungalow and the security of her room.

CHAPTER TEN

A GENTLE knock at the door roused Jo next morning and Jasmin came in, opened the louvre windows and set down a loaded tray by the bed. Jo, drugged from sleep, struggled to sit up.

'Good morning, madame. I hope you slept well.' She certainly spoke excellent English—even down to the Canadian accent.

'Yes, thank you, Jasmin, I did—very well.' Then Jo caught sight of the contents of the tray—orange juice, a plate full of croissants and hot rolls, English strawberry preserve and a silver pot of coffee. 'Goodness, I can't eat all that!'

The girl giggled. 'Mr Roker said that you——' she hesitated '——need feeding up and I was to make you eat. Your little boy already has his.'

When she had gone, Jo leaned back luxuriously against her pillows and slowly ate her breakfast. Absently, she watched the sunlight shaft through the louvres, making patterns on the blue-tiled floor, as a sensation of delicious ease began to seep through her whole body. Up to the day of their departure she had been caught up in a hectic whirl of preparations, and panic—even calling last-minute instructions to Bobbie through the car window as Adam drove away down the lane. But now Pear Trees really was beginning to feel half a world away.

By the time she was showered and in her housecoat, hesitating over what she should wear, Jon had appeared in shirt and swimming-trunks. 'Adam says, when you're

128

ready we're to come on round to the pool—everyone will be there.'

'Well, why don't you go on, love, and meet the other children? I saw them last night and they look very nice.'

'Oh, no, Mummy, let me wait for you. I'll read on my bed till you're ready.' And before she could argue, he was gone.

Jo smiled wryly to herself. Poor Jon—they both felt the same: slightly timid, apprehensive, even. Still, they couldn't skulk in their bedrooms all day. She hesitated, biting her lip, then fetched out the new, dark blue swimsuit she had bought in Broadston and wriggled into it. She hadn't worn it before and she looked critically at herself in the full-length glass. There was nothing exactly wrong with the swimsuit, but all the same . . . she began to think it might have been better to have indulged in one of the prettier but more expensive suits the assistant had shown her . . . and besides, she was definitely too thin, although she certainly wasn't going to admit as much to Adam. She covered her swimsuit with a loose-fitting smock dress and, picking up her bag and sunhat, went to collect Jon.

The pool was surrounded by more of the attractive lacy white walls and tall scented shrubs and they found their way to it, guided by shrieks and splashes. The three adults were sprawled on cane chairs under striped umbrellas on the small poolside terrace, while the children were rolling and tumbling in the turquoise-tiled pool like small brown porpoises. Jo felt Jon shrink closer to her side and she gave his shoulder a reassuring squeeze. The two men got up as they approached and Jo, unwilling to meet Adam's eyes, kept all her attention on Ali and Stella and the children, as they obediently hauled themselves out of the water to be introduced to Jon. But he stuck limpet-like to her side and seemed content just to watch the others as, after the rather wary hellos had been exchanged, they leapt back into the pool.

Stella, plumply comfortable in a loose but well-cut swimsuit, patted the upholstered chaise-longue on wheels alongside her. 'Come, Jo dear, have this—and don't feel you have to talk to us all morning. I expect you're still tired from the journey. I've brought a book and those two,' she pulled a face at Adam and Ali, 'will no doubt be talking shop.'

Jo, after a moment's hesitation, slipped out of the smock dress and, fishing out her suntan oil, began to smooth it over her skin.

'Oh, Jo—what a figure! I'm green with envy,' said Stella, although she didn't really look in the least envious. 'But—with those lovely long legs and slim waist, why don't you wear a bikini? Don't worry—it's quite all right to wear them in the privacy of our pool.'

'Thank you,' replied Jo stiffly, 'but I prefer a one-piece.'

'Oh, but you shouldn't, you really shouldn't,' Stella protested. 'Look, I'll tell you what—I've got a drawerful of bikinis which somehow I don't think I shall ever manage to squeeze myself into again.' She surveyed her plump curves with a complacent smile and as Jo began to protest politely she went on, 'I'll look some out for you later.'

She picked up her book and opened it, as though to prevent any further argument and, at the same time, Ali opened a slim attaché case and embarked on a lively discussion with Adam, so Jo finished oiling herself and Jon and then lay back on the chaise-longue. As she did so, she wondered for a moment how things were going at Pear Trees—perhaps she would give them a quick ring tomorrow, just to reassure herself that all was well. But as for today—Stella was right, she *was* tired. She closed her eyes and, still vaguely aware of the sounds around her—splashings and children's cries, Ali and Adam conversing—she drifted off into a light sleep.

At noon, they all retreated indoors, away from the

burning heat. She and Jon had a cold buffet lunch at a table laid on their veranda but she was grateful that Adam had gone off with Ali—she was disturbed enough, without his presence. Although he had spoken scarcely ten words to her and rarely seemed even to look in her direction the whole morning, she had been aware of him every moment of the time—his voice, quiet but forceful, breaking into her sleep, his body, lithe and tanned, as he joined Ali and the children for a quick bathe before lunch.

After their meal, Jon fetched a jigsaw and settled down happily with it on the veranda. Once he was engrossed, Jo went to her room, closed the shutters, making the room a dim cave, and lay down on the bed. When she woke, it was late afternoon and all residue of fatigue had gone, leaving her buoyant and refreshed. Both men were absent from dinner—Stella explained that they had driven down to Ali's office in Dhabra to examine some geological samples and would be very late. After dinner, Stella retired to bed, blaming the tiredness of early pregnancy, but not before she had pressed on Jo half a dozen bikinis. 'And mind you wear one tomorrow,' was her parting shot.

It was very late and Jo was all but asleep when there was a soft knock at her bedroom door and it opened. For a second she thought it was Jon, then through her lashes she made out a much larger outline and her body sprang into rigid wakefulness.

'Jo—are you awake?'

Above the pounding of her heart, she heard him cross the room towards the bed. He sat down on the edge of it and she could feel the hard muscles in his thigh against her arm, separated only by the thin sheet. She tried to move her arm away surreptitiously but it was trapped. The bed creaked as he leaned towards her and she felt the warmth of his body and smelt the faint tang of sweat.

'Jo.'

She couldn't pretend any longer. 'Mmm?' she murmured. Though she kept her eyes tightly closed, she could sense him, almost see him, his dark bulk bending over her. With horror, she remembered that under the single sheet she was naked, and mumbled again, 'Mmm?' trying at the same time to wriggle herself further into the flimsy security of the sheet. But the weight of Adam's body held it firmly and she only succeeded in rolling up against him.

'While I was in Ali's office I took the chance to ring Pear Trees.'

She sat up, remembering too late that she really shouldn't, and clutched the sheet to her. She heard Adam give a soft chuckle.

'I somehow thought the magic password of "Pear Trees" might rouse you from your slumbers where my magnetic presence failed.'

'But are they all right—are they coping?'

'Well—the kitchen's caught fire, the cellar's flooded—oh, and Bobbie's broken her leg. Otherwise, everything's fine.'

'Oh, for heaven's sake!' In spite of her exasperation Jo smiled, but then, feeling the sheet begin to slip again, she yanked it up under her chin and lay down quickly.

'Seriously—I thought you would be wondering. There are no problems—they were just getting organised for the evening. Bobbie sends her love and says don't do anything she wouldn't—mind you, knowing that young lady, I should think that would give you quite as much scope as you'd want.'

Jo, every nerve-ending in her body quivering, could not trust herself to reply and Adam went on, his voice gently caressing her, 'Of course, now I've woken you up, it does seem such a waste of a desirable naked body, just to let you turn over and go back to sleep.'

'Desirable? I'm the skinny one—remember?'

He laughed softly. 'Skinny you may be—but that doesn't stop you being highly desirable.'

Jo stared at him through the glimmering darkness. 'Go away, Adam—go away. You—you'll wake Jon.'

He lifted one hand and she flinched, but he only rested it on her head for a moment. 'Relax, Jo—nobody's going to eat you.' He bent towards her, so that she felt his warm breath on her tingling skin, then dropped a light kiss on her cheek. 'See you in the morning.' And he was gone.

After breakfast next morning, Jo agonised over what she should wear. She knew she would feel much happier in her own swimsuit but didn't want to offend Stella. Still, there was one bikini—a very pretty pink gingham, which was slightly less brief than the rest ... It certainly suited her figure, emphasising the fullness of her breasts and the slender curve of her hips ... Yes, she decided unwillingly that perhaps she had better wear it.

She had just put it on, when Jon came bursting in and bounced on to the bed. He eyed her appreciatively. 'Ooh, Mummy, you look great!'

Jo laughed, not sure whether to be pleased or not. 'Well, thank you, love,' she said.

'Have you finished your breakfast? Can I have this?' Jon picked up a large brioche and began cramming it into his mouth as Jo looked at him in amazement—was this the child who usually had to be cajoled at every meal to eat more than the absolute minimum?

'I've been to see Ranji's train set,' he announced. 'He came to fetch me when I was having my breakfast. Oh, and did you know he's a prince? His train set's marvellous—he let me change the points and operate——'

'What did you say, Jon? He's a prince?'

'Oh yes—he told me. But it doesn't bother him. His

father's a prince as well,' he added. 'Hurry up, Mummy, let's get round to the pool,' and he was off the bed and hovering by the door.

But Jo was still trying to gather her whirling thoughts. Ali—a prince! Why on earth hadn't Adam told her? Was she supposed to have guessed? Maybe she should have done—that air of self-confidence, of easy affluence. And yet, how could she have been expected to know? Her mind flicked rapidly through the previous day, wondering if she had made too much of a fool of herself. Once again, she felt that odd twinge of jealousy at the thought of the three of them, cosy in their relationship, while she was an outsider. But then, she asked herself, whose fault is it if you *are* an outsider?

Jo had hoped to be ahead of the others this morning but they were already there, Adam playing with a beachball in the water with the children. When she slipped off her cover-up Ali eyed her up and down appreciatively. 'Very nice, Jo.'

Stella scowled at him. 'What a nerve. He gives me five—no six children, and then starts making eyes at you—and in *my* bikini!' But she smiled broadly at her husband and winked at Jo, who settled down on the chaise longue.

After a moment's hesitation, Jon sat beside her, watching the others. Adam hurled the ball towards the far end of the pool, swung himself out of the water and came towards them purposefully, shaking the water out of his hair. Before Jon could escape, Adam had snatched him up and dropped him—very gently—into the shallow end of the pool. Jon, red-faced and spluttering, struggled to his feet, looking as though he was about to launch himself into a violent rage. Jo's stomach contracted in alarm, but just then two-year old Leila called 'Jon, Jon,' and splashed across the pool in her white plastic swan ring, and he dog-paddled towards her.

Jo oiled herself and lay back, eyes closed, feeling weak with relief. Stella and her husband were talking quietly, their voices almost drowned by the shouts from the pool—Jon's among them. The sun was hot on her face and she soon rolled over on to her stomach. After a few minutes, she sensed a movement beside her, then felt suntan oil being dribbled on to her shoulders and back.

'Mmm, thank you, Stella,' she murmured, then realised that the hands rhythmically massaging her skin were not Stella's.

Instinctively she tightened up and Adam's voice breathed in her ear, 'Take it easy, Jo. You don't want to get sunburned, do you?'

The light touch of his fingers was electrifying her senses and she turned her head away so that he wouldn't see the colour creeping up her cheeks. She willed herself to lie as rigid as a board while he methodically smoothed the oil over her hot skin. As he finished, she remembered something. Groping for her sunglasses, she put them on and sat up, so that their faces were on a level.

'Why didn't you tell me?' she demanded, keeping her voice low.

He guessed immediately what she meant and shrugged. 'You didn't ask me.'

'Why on earth should I have done?' she hissed. 'And anyway, you said Ali was a petroleum engineer.'

'So he is—just about the best in the country. And he has to work for his living, you know—the family believe in making full use of his talents. Anyway, does it matter? It doesn't to him—and, in any case, he's a fairly minor prince—he's got a couple of dozen older brothers!'

'But you should have warned me.'

'You were in such a tizzy before we left England that I was afraid if I told you, you'd have gone clear into orbit. I thought it would be better for you to find out for yourself, once you were safely out here.'

'Maybe, but——' she began, but just then Jon called to Adam and he stood up and walked across to the pool.

Jo watched him go and, despite her still simmering hostility, found herself objectively surveying his body—the broad shoulders and powerful chest, tapering to slim waist and hips. What a good physique he has, she thought idly, muscular but controlled. She blushed as she realised the track her musings were taking her, then flushed even more as she saw that he had turned and was watching her, his gaze seeming to penetrate her thoughts, as she rolled hastily on to her stomach once more.

The next week passed in a lazy, pampered blur—days spent by the pool, in the pool, eating, chatting with Stella. Sometimes Adam was there; more often, he and Ali were missing. This suited Jo for, whenever he was around, she was on edge. Underneath, she was still resentful at the way he had so skilfully won the argument over the trip and, although she managed to maintain a plausible façade of politeness when they were in company, even a certain amount of counterfeit warmth, she congratulated herself that she had avoided any more occasions of being really alone with him.

Besides, she could never forget her main reason for being there. Whenever Adam was playing with the children she was on guard, watchful in case he gave a second's more attention to Jon. It was true that Adam seemed to treat him with scrupulous impartiality but nonetheless, Jo sensed a constant undercurrent of emotion in his dealings with his son—and Jon's eager yet unwitting response to this.

Now, she glanced across at Jon, playing football by the pool with Ranji—suntanned, his hair bleached gold. Almost magically, he had lost the withdrawn look, his face was filling out and he looked more robust, more confident.

As she watched, Ranji snatched the ball away from him and he went sprawling. He got to his feet, rubbing his elbow angrily and frowning in her direction. But then, as Jo quailed inwardly, he threw himself on the other boy and they tumbled over into the pool, like a pair of frolicking puppies.

Stella caught her eye and smiled. 'Jon and Ranji have really hit it off, haven't they? It's so good for Ranji to have someone of his own age to play with—and Jon is such a nice boy.'

Stella's face was open and guileless, but the subject of Jon was uneasy ground for Jo—she still wasn't sure how much Adam had told them—so she only smiled and leaned back under her umbrella. She stretched herself luxuriously.

'Goodness, how lazy I feel. You know Stella, I've seen absolutely nothing of Rabbaq since we arrived—I've almost taken root in this chair. I suppose I really should try——'

'But Jo, I've just had a wonderful idea.' Stella bounced upright. 'In a few days' time, Ali is taking Adam to a new oil-drilling area in the north. You can go with them.'

'Oh, I don't——' Jo began, but Stella waved her hand impatiently.

'Yes, yes—and, even better, there's the ruins of an ancient city not far off the route. It's called Qatrak—it's a pretty spot, by an oasis. Do go, Jo—you'll love it. There won't be room for Jon—they'll only be able to squeeze you in, I'm afraid—but he'll be happier here with us anyway.'

Jo could only give in gracefully, although the thought of such close proximity to Adam, even with Ali as a barrier between them, was disturbing, and she was glad that he had gone off into town again that morning. She would be able to compose her face before he heard of the plan—although, of course, there was every chance that he would be no better pleased to have her along than she was to go with them.

That afternoon, as usual, she settled Jon in his room for a rest then lay down on her own bed, glad to be out of the merciless glare of heat. She lay wakeful at first, staring at the ceiling in the subdued light that filtered through the closed louvres, but then at length she drifted off to sleep.

When she came to, the light had changed so she knew it must be quite late afternoon. She opened her door and called, 'Jon, time to get up' but there was no reply. He must be flat out, she thought with a smile, worn out by the morning's exertions, so she went into his room. But it was empty; Jon was not there. She went out and stood on the veranda, listening, but no sounds came from the direction of the pool. She called, 'Jasmin', then remembered that the girl went to her own home after lunch. Finally, she knocked tentatively on Adam's bedroom door, but there was no response.

There was no sign of Jon anywhere in the garden either, and the pool, as she had expected, lay empty, its surface smooth and unruffled, with that blank look that only a deserted swimming-pool has. She went back to the bungalow and walked restlessly along the passage and through the dim, silent rooms. Keep calm, she told herself, he won't have wandered off into the hills alone, he just wouldn't. Perhaps he had gone off somewhere with Ranji— but Stella would have made sure that she was told first. She glanced at her watch—she didn't want to alarm anyone unnecessarily, but it *was* past five o'clock. In little more than an hour, it would be dark ...

She had just made up her mind that she must go across to Stella's bungalow and try to contact Adam by phone, when a car swept round the corner and drew up at the foot of the steps—and she saw that the driver was Adam. Thank heavens! Her heart lifted as she hurried towards the veranda steps. And then she saw that he was not alone—

beside him was Jon. She stopped dead, waiting, as the boy got out.

'Mummy, Mummy. You'll never guess where we've been!'

His face was radiant. He never looks like that with me, thought Jo, involuntarily.

'Jon——'

'We've been to the zoo! Adam took me to the zoo. We've seen Bengal tigers—and a giant panda!'

'To the zoo?' she repeated stupidly.

'Yes—it was great!'

He threw himself at Adam, hugging him round the waist and squealing with delight as he was thrown high in the air. Adam set him on his feet, ruffled his hair and smiled down at him, and at the expressions on their faces Jo was forced to lean against the veranda rail to steady herself. Her momentary relief at seeing Jon was engulfed by a suffocating wave of jealousy as her deepest fears were confirmed. Despite all her vigilance, Adam had slipped under her guard and was weaving his glittering spell around the boy. With terrifying clarity, she had a vision of Jon being drawn further and further away from her—and she was absolutely powerless to prevent it.

As she put out an ineffectual hand to grab him, Jon darted past her. 'I must go and change, Mummy. There's just time for a swim before supper.'

'Don't be long,' she called mechanically at his retreating back.

Adam, apparently quite unaware that anything was wrong, came up the steps, smiling at her. She regarded him, flint-faced. 'How dare you take Jon off without telling me.'

His smile faded, to be replaced by a look of resigned patience that infuriated her even more.

'I looked in on you but you were sound asleep and looking very—comfortable. It seemed a pity to disturb you—although if Jon hadn't been around, I might have been tempted.'

But he had miscalculated for once and, impervious to his tone, she merely retorted, 'You shouldn't have taken him, then. I d-didn't know where he'd gone.' Her voice shook slightly.

'And so I suppose that quicksilver mind of yours had him wandering off into the desert, never to be seen again. Oh, Jo——' He shook his head at her and went to put his hand on her shoulder but she shrugged him off and stepped back from him.

'Don't you "Oh, Jo" me,' she snapped.

Adam stood, frowning for a moment, then he dropped on to a cane sofa. 'Sit down, Jo.' His voice was peremptory. 'We've got to have this out, and now's as good a chance as any.'

She hesitated, then sat down on the extreme edge of the sofa, not looking at him. 'Once and for all, Adam, I won't have you interfering—taking Jon off without asking me. You should have waited. I wouldn't have tried to stop you taking him—he's never been to a zoo.'

'Well, it isn't actually a zoo—more a haven for endangered species that's just been set up on the outskirts of Dhabra.'

Jo sat, staring at the ground, then suddenly tensed as she felt his hand close on hers. She tried to wrench away, but he held her in a grip of steel.

'Listen to me, Jo.' He spoke slowly, as though feeling for every word. 'I must make you understand somehow. Whatever happens in the future, whatever I may want to do—can do—for Jon, nothing can possibly blot out his first seven years, when you were everything to him—and I wouldn't want it to, either. Look at me.'

He turned her head gently towards him, so that she was forced to look into his eyes. 'Jon worships you—why, he's hardly stopped talking about you all afternoon! He absolutely adores you—and that will never change. In years to come, when he's older, he'll grow away from you—it's inevitable and it's only right that he should. But I know that you will always hold a special place in his heart.' He paused, then went on, 'I've done many things to you, Jo, but I shall never take Jon from you. Did you really think I would?'

When she didn't reply, he gave a twisted smile. 'Well, I suppose it's only what I deserve, that you should always think the worst of me. But did you really think I would?'

'Yes, yes, I did—at least, I was terribly afraid that it would happen——'

'And now——' he prompted gently.

At first, no words came and Jo sat silent. Finally, she looked up once more. The urgent sincerity of his voice was mirrored in the deep concern in his eyes as, hardly breathing, he watched her. At last her lips trembled into a half-smile and she whispered, 'No'. Just one word, but it was enough—enough to melt the hard core of her jealous and possessive love. It was as though the infection which had festered secretly in her mind for months had come to a painful, throbbing head—and now Adam had lanced it and all the poison was oozing away.

She took a deep breath, then smiled again. It was the first time for eight years that she had really smiled at him, not only with her lips but with her eyes, and Adam's breath caught in his throat. He cupped her face with his hands, then bent his head and, with infinite gentleness, brushed her lips in the softest of kisses which sent tingles of electricity prickling along her nerve ends.

At last, his mouth slid from hers, to trail light caressing kisses across the line of her throat, then on round the low curve of her sundress neckline until he reached the swell of her breasts. Her heart was bounding wildly as she felt his breath warm against her flesh. Then, as he raised his head momentarily, she saw the flame of lambent passion in his eyes and, with a sickening lurch of panic, she jerked up her hands to thrust him away from her.

'No, Adam, no,' she said sharply. 'Jon will be back.'

He straightened up, breathing fast.

'OK, Jo, it's all right—the beast's quite under control, I promise.' He got to his feet, as though eager to distance himself from her. 'I'd better get ready for dinner.'

When he had gone, Jo sat where she was, smoothing back her hair with hands which were not quite steady. Although it was perfectly true—Jon *was* likely to return at any second—she knew deep down that this was not why she had drawn back in such sudden abhorrence. No—the old fears, the long-buried memories, had fought their way to the surface of her consciousness once more and once again she had been totally unable to stop them.

CHAPTER ELEVEN

THE carved wardrobe in Jo's room was so cavernous that her clothes occupied only one end and she riffled through them, her heart sinking.

'Don't worry about the reception,' Stella had told her airily. 'It's just a little get-together for a few friends. Ali wants Adam to meet some of the locals that he doesn't already know, so while they talk boring old shop, you and I can have a hen party with their wives.'

All the same, *little* get-together or not, Jo had felt distinctly apprehensive. She could just imagine how chic and elegant Stella's 'few friends' would turn out to be. In self-defence, she would have to spend some time on her appearance, and with Jon out with Ranji for the afternoon, she had the place to herself.

She returned to the problem of what she was to wear. There were only two possibilities and she laid them side by side on the bed—the lightweight jersey two-piece, or an oldish but still attractive long cotton skirt in a muted jade/navy stripe, with a plain jade top. Yes, that would be best—not ideal perhaps but it would do. She put the two-piece away, undressed and went through to the bathroom, reflecting wryly as she did so that it would be a novel experience for her to devote an entire long, sybaritic afternoon solely to her own appearance. For years, she had happily polished the Pear Trees' silver until she could see her face and hair in it, while giving that same face and hair the most perfunctory of attention, just sufficient to keep herself looking neat and well-groomed for the restaurant.

Someone—Stella no doubt—had equipped the bath-room with a small regiment of bottles and jars of luxurious beauty preparations. Jo shampooed her hair, slapped conditioner on it and put on a face pack, before relaxing into the heady perfume of a warm, gardenia-scented bubblebath. Afterwards, she rubbed matching skin-oil over every inch of her body and sat, golden and glowing, on the veranda, wrapped in a bath towel, while her hair dried.

Later, seated at her dressing-table and studying her reflection critically, Jo couldn't resist a faint, almost shy smile of approval at the face which gazed back at her. Her tanned skin had a faint sheen which set off her delicate features, making the green of her eyes more vivid and intense, so that all she needed to do was enhance their colour further with a soft jade eye-shadow, brush along the sweep of her lashes with brown mascara and colour her lips with a soft yet vibrant coral lip-gloss.

Her hair, thanks to the sun and Stella's conditioner, hung on her shoulders in skeins of gold silk. Automatically, she began to comb it up into one hand to twist it into its familiar knot, but then she stopped, letting it slip through her fingers again so that it framed her face. It would be such a pity to imprison it tonight in a fortress of hair grips and spray! Her heart beating rather fast at her own temerity, Jo combed it through again, teased out a few of the front strands in soft wisps against her face, and left the rest to hang straight.

She had just finished when there was a knock at the door and Jasmin came in, all smiles and carrying a large white box. 'Mr Roker asked me to give you this.'

She set the box down on the bed and stood back, her small brown face alight with eager curiosity. Jo's fingers fumbled with the silver string and, very slowly, almost unwillingly, she lifted the lid and parted the tissue paper inside. 'Oh,' she breathed in wonderment and half lifted out the shimmering silk dress with hands become suddenly stiff and clumsy.

The two of them looked at each other, round eyed, then Jo stood up, shaking out the folds of silk. It was simply the most beautiful dress she had ever set eyes on—the silk was feather-light, cream, almost parchment colour, and shot through with a subtle, iridescent gold thread. It was perfectly decorous, with a high neckline and long slim sleeves, and the style couldn't have been simpler, but Jo was under no illusion as to how much Adam must have paid for it. She couldn't accept it—it would be a dreadful mistake. Mechanically, she began to fold the beautiful thing back into its box.

'Oh, madame—are you not going to wear the dress?'

Jo looked up, startled—she had almost forgotten Jasmin was there. 'No, I—I don't think so——' she said.

'But—madame, it is so beautiful,' the girl said tremulously.

Jo saw the wistfulness in her eyes and a feeling of shame smote her. This young girl, who would never in all her life be able to afford a dress a hundredth part as lovely as this one, just wanted the unselfish pleasure of seeing her in it, and Jo knew all at once that she must wear it.

She smiled. 'Put the other clothes away, Jasmin—and you can help me dress, if you like.'

The dress slipped down over her like a second skin, fitting perfectly—almost too perfectly, thought Jo, as she surveyed herself in the full-length mirror whilst Jasmin did up the tiny silk-covered buttons down the back and she saw the line of the dress fall from the high swell of her breasts, down over the curve of her hips and lower back. She shook her head at the reflection, smiling to herself—was it really her, this soft, glowing, beautiful creature? Creation, more like, she told herself sternly—the product of a horrendously expensive dressmaker and a thoroughly self-indulgent afternoon!

When she went out on to the veranda, Adam, in a dark lightweight suit, and Jon were ensconced in cane chairs, talking, and she hesitated in the doorway for a moment. When they saw her, they both got to their feet, watching her as she walked across to them, her heart beating erratically. She found she couldn't look at Adam at all so she fixed her attention on Jon, who was gaping at her.

She smiled at him. 'Hello, love. Have you had a nice afternoon?'

'Mummy, you look——'

He stopped and Adam put his hand on the boy's shoulder. 'Yes, she does, doesn't she,' and their eyes met over Jon's head for an instant.

Of the three, Jon was the first to recover, and he gave his mother a quick hug. 'I'm having supper with Ranji—we've been out into the desert in the Land Rover, looking for gerbils. 'Bye.' And he was gone.

Jo watched him out of sight, then, avoiding Adam's eyes, she said, 'I thought gerbils lived in cages.'

'So they do—a good many of them. But there are still plenty running around out here.'

She stood twisting the silk between her fingers nervously, very conscious of the last occasion she had been alone with him.

'Thank you—for the dress.' She darted a look at him from under her lashes.

'Thank you for wearing it,' he replied gravely. 'I half thought you wouldn't. And in case you're wondering, Stella saw to it.'

'Oh.' An absurd sense of disappointment swept over her—so all he had done was foot the bill.

But then he went on. 'At least, she saw to all the important things—I gather she sneaked one of your dresses, with Jasmin's help, to get your size—correctly, I imagine, to judge from the result.' She felt his eyes travel slowly down her body. 'And her dressmaker made it. The only thing I can lay claim to is choosing the material, alone and unaided. I hope you like my choice—I thought it would set off your suntan and hair. And I was right.'

Her gaze locked with his, quite unable to tear itself free, until he went on, his voice tight, 'I suppose we'd better go—the cars have been arriving for the last half-hour.'

As though by tacit agreement, they walked through the gardens in silence and well apart, the only sounds their footsteps crunching softly on the gravel, and the faint swish of the silk against her legs.

At Stella and Ali's bungalow several of the cane screens between the rooms had been drawn back to make a huge open-plan area, extending on to the veranda, where strings of coloured lights had been hung, as well as candles in elegant glass bowls. They walked in together and Jo was glad she wasn't on her own, as dozens of pairs of eyes turned in their direction. The women were merely curious, but she sensed speculative, appreciative glances from the dark-suited or white-robed men, standing around in small, private masculine groups. Then Stella descended on her and she was taken over to be introduced to a bevy of women, fully as elegant and smoothly glamorous as she had expected.

Mostly, Jo was content to sit quietly, making polite conversation when needed, but otherwise a spectator of the noisy, colourful scene. The buffet, laid in an inner room, was quite sensational and Jo loaded her plate and retired to the women's corner to enjoy the feast. Her eyes strayed frequently towards where the men were sitting, but each time she found Adam's eyes on her, and each time she hastily withdrew her own, but not before she felt an intangible thread of tension between them tighten a little more. All evening, the consciousness of his presence stayed with her: she chatted, thinking of him; she ate, thinking of him; and she sipped her chilled fruit juice without tasting it.

By eleven, the guests had begun drifting away and Jo, after a quick goodnight to Stella, went too. She knew that she ought to wait for Adam who had, after all, escorted her to the reception, but all at once she felt an urgent need to seek the safe refuge of her room. She was already half-way along the path to the guest bungalow when she heard his voice calling her. Her stride faltered, then she reluctantly turned to face him as he came up to her, in no apparent haste.

'You're in quite a hurry. Why didn't you wait?'

'Oh, I—I thought you were still busy talking shop,' she said lamely.

He put his hand firmly on her elbow and drew her off the path, down a side walk through the gardens. 'We'll go this way, I think.'

There were candles fixed to posts, flickering among the sweet-scented shrubs, to guide them but above their heads the sky was inky black, lit only by pinpricks of stars and bursts of light as cars pulled away down the mountain road. Adam kept his hand under her elbow, deliberately slowing her pace, his fingers gripping her tightly, so that she was forced to stay very much closer to him than she wanted.

'I haven't told you yet how very beautiful you look tonight—the most stunning girl in the place.'

'Thank you—Stella's dressmaker would no doubt be highly gratified to hear you.'

Despite her flippant tone, Jo knew that her nervousness was betrayed in her voice and she tried to quicken the pace, but Adam stopped in the dense shade of a clump of palms and turned her to face him squarely.

'Jo, don't keep running away from me.' His voice was quite steady but she sensed the tension behind the words.

'I'm hardly running away from you at the moment,' she said lightly, but he shook her impatiently.

'You know very well what I mean. You're retreating from me all the time, trying to keep Jon, Stella—anybody, between us.'

'Oh, really, Adam. You're rather letting your imagination run riot, aren't you?'

But even as she spoke, with him looming over her in the darkness, she knew that it was true. She had been running away from Adam ever since they had arrived in Rabbaq— and she also knew, with a pulsebeat of fear, that this time there was no possibility of reprieve by Jon, or anyone else.

'Please let me go,' she began, but as she tried to break away from him he pulled her to him and his mouth came down on hers, silencing her momentarily. In her fear of him, she tried to struggle free, twisting her head away and gasping, 'Please, Adam, no—it's no use—I can't——' but he only plucked her off her feet and held her against one of the palms. He put his hands each side of her, imprisoning her securely against the rough bark, and began to kiss her again, but this time very slowly and gently.

At first, she still tried to fight against him, but finally, under the lingering, honeyed touch of his lips, and almost without her realising it, her own lips opened and his tongue began to probe her mouth with an infinite delicacy. And then, with a sense of incredulous relief, Jo felt her fear almost imperceptibly begin to ease its grip. With a tiny sigh, she closed her eyes and slipped her arms around him.

Through the soft silk of her dress she sensed his hands move to her body, caressing the rounded contours of her hips then slowly sliding upwards to brush lightly, tantalisingly, against her breasts. Under the touch of his fingers, Jo felt her body quiver. Entirely new, delicate sensations rippled through her until, hardly breathing, she realised that, miraculously, she didn't want Adam to stop, she wanted him to go on loving her like this for ever.

But then, even as the thought entered her consciousness, his hands slid round her back and his fingers were fumbling with the tiny silk-covered buttons. Despite his gentleness, Jo felt herself stiffen against him and she gave a stifled gasp, but he only lifted his head for an instant and whispered,' It's all right, my darling, it's all right—I won't hurt you.'

His other hand moved down her spine, he clasped her even more tightly to him, and she felt his body taut against hers. With a numbing horror, Jo felt the insidious spiral of panic begin to spin deep inside her. Frantically, she fought to conquer it, but it continued to force its way upwards until it rose to a shuddering climax of despair which overwhelmed and obliterated all other emotions.

Abruptly, she jerked herself away, there was a harsh, tearing sound, the fabric ripped and she felt his hands on her bare shoulder. Terror flared out—she tore herself free and backed up against the palm, trembling, as the stars reeled dizzily over her head. She was thrusting him away with all her strength, saying over and over, 'No, Adam, no, no,' until at last his hands dropped to his sides and he stood quite still, looking down at her through the darkness. He was breathing very hard as though he had been running, and he leaned his shoulder against the tree, his face a pale blur against the deeper shadow. Jo, shivering violently, tried to draw up the torn neckline of her ruined dress.

'I—I'm sorry, Adam.' Her lips were trembling so that she could hardly get the words out. 'It was all my fault—not yours.' The voice was so racked with anguish that she could hardly recognise it as her own. 'I—I thought——' She bit her lip, fighting for control, as a hiccuping sob burst out. She clapped both hands to her mouth to smother it but then, as Adam moved towards her, as though to take her in his arms, she broke away and, still holding her hands to her mouth, ran headlong down the path in search of sanctuary.

Jasmin had opened the louvres in the bedroom and the cold, brilliant moonlight shafted across the tiled floor like the bars of an enclosing prison. Jo tore off her clothes and threw herself on the bed. The sobs which she had fought to stifle burst out, tearing at her body, and she buried her head against the pillow, quite unable to stop the dreadful, retching gasps.

When the door opened, she was still crying, so she did not hear someone come in and close the door softly. Nor was she even aware of someone sitting down on the edge of the bed. Only when a hand began gently stroking her tangled hair did she look up, startled. In the moonlight, Adam's face was a pale, strained mask, his eyes brooding as he looked down at her. Jo, conscious that she was naked, gave a convulsive start and curled her body protectively.

She turned her back again, gasping, 'Oh, g-go away— just leave me alone, will you,' but he continued to sit, softly stroking her hair. In spite of herself, the gently rhythmic action began to soothe her until finally she gave a long, quivering sigh and then lay still. He took out his handkerchief and wiped her swollen eyes and blotched cheeks, then bending over her, his voice soft but urgent, he said, 'Jo, tell me why you were crying—why you were *so* upset.'

Oh, God, she thought wearily, not a post-mortem now— I can't bear it. She moved her head restlessly against the pillow, too emotionally exhausted now even to attempt to hide her body from him. Aloud, she said, a catch in her throat, 'I d-don't know.'

With his little finger, Adam traced the shining course of one fresh tear down her cheek. Very patiently, as though speaking to a recalcitrant child, he repeated, 'Please tell me, Jo. Why were you crying?'

There was a long silence, then at length she whispered, 'I thought I wanted you to kiss me. I w-wanted to respond, but it's no good—I c-can't.' Her lips quivered and she tried to smile up at him, a wan, pale little smile. 'I tried—I tried so hard. And I thought, I really thought—but, then——'

He drew a deep breath, then lifted her hand to his lips and kissed each finger softly. 'Thank you for telling me. It can't have been easy, but I had to make you admit it to yourself.' His smile was ragged. 'Jo——.' He hesitated so long that finally she looked up at him enquiringly. 'Jo—there hasn't been anyone else, has there?' It was a statement, not a question. 'I thought at first that you and Sinclair, with his "Jo this" and "Jo that"—I could have killed him with my bare hands—but he's nothing to you, is he?'

Jo began mechanically picking at his shirt buttons, feeling the warm solidity of the man under the fine cotton. 'No.'

'In other words—it's all my fault. Oh, don't try to argue—we both know it is. I'm the one who's done this to you. So, OK—we'll just have to go right back to the beginning again—back to square one. And I'll wait—twenty years, if need be. You'll find that I'm a *very* patient man.'

He grinned at her lopsidedly but she burst out, 'Oh, Adam—stop fooling yourself! You're wasting your time. Please—just leave me alone.' In her anxiety to make him understand, to save him—and herself—needless pain, she seized a handful of his shirt and shook it in emphasis. 'I don't want to hurt you—not now—really, I don't. When you first came back, I did—I wanted to tear you apart, make you suffer—but that's gone now. I just feel empty.' Her voice was desolate. 'So, you must believe me, Adam, it's not twenty years—it's never. I just know it.'

He put his hand softly over her mouth and shook his head at her, a tenderness in his eyes that made her heart twist for an instant. But all he said was, 'We'll see.'

Well, thought Jo, I've tried to warn him, save him from grief, but if he persists . . .

'Apart from anything else,' he continued, 'it's such a waste of a lovely body.' She felt his eyes slowly, yet without threat, range over her body as he murmured, his voice catching, 'You're like a white marble statue in some mysterious moonlit garden—beautiful, untouched.'

He brought up his hand and laid it lightly across her stomach, his fingers splayed against her skin, but Jo lay quiescent, knowing that he would not harm her. He looked up at her and, surprised, she saw the pain in his eyes.

'What's the matter?'

'I was just wishing—wishing that I'd been around when you were pregnant. You must have been so beautiful then—rounded, fulfilled.'

'Hardly that.' Her face was ravaged. 'I looked terrible— not at all your average blooming young mother.' She tried to speak lightly, but there was an ache behind the words. 'You'd have thought me ugly, I'm sure.'

His hands moved gently against her skin. 'Never—when you were carrying my child, your body would have been more lovely, more precious to me——'

Jo rolled away from him, quite unable to bear any more. 'I'm very tired—please go now.'

Her voice was muffled and she bit her lip, afraid that a

stray sob might sneak out. Adam stood up and pulled the sheet over her.

Trying to keep her voice cool, she went on, 'I'll let you in on Jon as much as you like—I know he needs you. But that's all.' She watched as he closed the louvres, then spoke into the sudden dark. 'As to what I said earlier—we can share *our* son, but we can't be anything more to each other. Maybe, once we might have been—but not now—it's eight years too late.'

CHAPTER TWELVE

To Jo's eyes, as the Land Rover turned off the tarmac highway down a rutted road, the desert seemed limitless, stretching away to a shimmering horizon. They had left in the pre-dawn cool, but now the sun had risen and was blazing through the windscreen. Jo, squeezed between the two men, felt a trickle of sweat run down her back, and her thighs, even though she was wearing loose cotton trousers, were sticky. Also, the swaying, bouncing motion of the vehicle was making her quite queasy.

Adam, sensing her discomfort, let his eyes stray briefly from the road ahead, to her, then he spoke over her head to Ali. 'We'll have a break at the next town, if you like—I could show Jo the *souq*.'

They arrived at the 'town'—a few dozen low white, flat-roofed houses on each side of the dusty road—and Adam parked in the meagre shade of a clump of palms. The *souq* had a surprisingly wide range of items for sale in the open-fronted shops—Adam told her that the town was on a route still used by nomadic tribesmen and some of them were very wealthy. She easily found presents for the staff—a Turkish coffee-pot in beaten copper for Phil, a finely embroidered silk scarf for Daphne and then, in a tiny shop hardly bigger than a cupboard, perfume for Bobbie. She watched, fascinated, in the heady, scented air, as the shopkeeper decanted the jasmine into a glass vial, then left Adam buying perfume for his sister.

After the scene with Adam following the reception, Jo had been strongly tempted to duck out of the excursion, but

155

she knew that any excuse would have sounded feeble, even ungracious, to Stella and even more so to Ali. Besides, she genuinely did not want to leave Rabbaq without seeing at least a little of the country—and, after all, Ali would be there the whole time to act as an unwitting buffer between them.

She wandered to the far end of the narrow, dark alley, where she came to an Aladdin's cave—or so it seemed—a stall selling gold jewellery. Much of the gold looked thin and of poor quality, but even Jo's inexperienced eyes were able to pick out a few very fine pieces. She pulled one necklace out from a tangled mass and held it up. It was a long rope of polished amber ovals, each set in a small fretted gold cup and joined together by heavy gold medallions. In the soft light it was quite superb, with the sort of rare beauty that would have graced the neck of some barbarian chieftain's bride.

'It's beautiful—would you like it?' Adam was beside her. 'Let me buy it for you—a souvenir of Rabbaq.'

Jo was horrified. 'Oh, no—no, thank you.'

She set it down, smiling regret at the young boy in charge of the stall, and when Adam put his hand on it she said firmly, 'No, please don't, Adam. Thank you—but I'd much rather you didn't.'

Her voice was more stilted than she had intended—chilly, even—and the memory of the night of the reception hung in the air between them. She walked purposefully away to rejoin Ali, leaving Adam to follow her.

The oil-exploration site was way out in the desert. A collection of prefabricated bungalows were ranged round a central compound, where some attempt had been made to create a garden, with shrubs and a square of dusty brown grass. Some distance away there was a rough platform of scaffolding, over machinery which whined and clanked.

Ali took Jo into one of the bungalows and told a manservant to look after her, then he and Adam disappeared.

The servant showed her to a modern bathroom, and she peeled off her clothes and showered. The water in the shower, like everything else out here, was slightly brown but, still, it was cool and refreshing. On the small shaded veranda there were comfortable chairs and a pile of newspapers and magazines, only a couple of weeks old. At lunchtime the servant appeared with lamb kebabs and rice and a bowl of fruit, and when she had eaten them, Jo, lulled by the distant hum of machinery, fell into a light sleep.

She woke as a battered truck pulled up under the veranda and Ali and Adam climbed out. They both looked very tired and strained, but Ali spared her an apologetic smile.

'Jo, I'm sorry, but I shan't be able to return with you. We've struck problems in getting our pumps down through the rock and I must stay and sort things out. But Adam will take you to see Qatrak on your way back to Dhabra. So I'm afraid it's goodbye, Jo—and safe journey.'

Aghast, Jo stared up at him for a second, then she somehow got to her feet, her knees trembling slightly.

'Thank you, Ali—for Jon and myself. We've both had a wonderful holiday.' She was pleased that she sounded quite composed.

'I hope we shall have the pleasure of seeing you again soon?' His eyes were intent on hers and, with Adam just a few feet away, she felt quite unable to answer his implicit question. She smiled at him and held out her hand.

'Goodbye, Ali—and thank you, again.'

As the truck roared off, spurting dust from under its wheels, the servant appeared with a tray of tea. Adam gulped down two cups then looked at his watch and stood up.

'Time for off, I'm afraid—I'd rather not be caught out in the desert at nightfall.'

Without a word, Jo followed him to the Land Rover and climbed in. At least without Ali there was more room, and she perched as far away from Adam as possible, one shoulder pressed hard against the vehicle's side. For the first half-hour, she sat in silence as Adam negotiated the difficult road, only occasionally sneaking glances at him. This was a very different Adam from the suave, immaculate man she had grown used to. His clothes—an old shirt and shorts—were filthy, and he smelt faintly of sweat and sun. His unshaven face and hands were grimed with grease and dust, while his dark hair was finely powdered over with the same pale dust. He at once looked more familiar and yet more remote than she had seen him for years, and as she risked another glance at the stern, withdrawn profile, her heart seemed to leap under her ribs, pounding so that she could hardly breathe for a heady mixture of excitement and apprehension.

She was still wondering what on earth was the matter with her when, at that moment, sensing her eyes upon him, he turned and looked at her, his eyes holding hers for a few seconds, until she tore hers away, a scalding, burning wave of heat bursting all over her body. She stared out of the window, her head turned away from him, watching the flat, barren emptiness slide past her.

When the silence had gone on for too long, she cleared her throat and said, in as normal a voice as she could manage, 'I'm sorry you had to leave to bring me—I expect you'd rather have stayed.'

'Oh, I have to be back in the UK in a couple of days, anyway. And I know you wanted to see Qatrak. Besides,

I'm——' He broke off abruptly, and she didn't prompt him to continue.

They came to a crossroads and Adam turned off the dusty road on to a rough track. 'Hold on to your inside—this is where things get interesting,' he said, and for the next fifteen miles or so they slithered and skidded over deep ruts, round huge boulders and across a wide, dried-up river bed, where the few remaining patches of shiny mud made the going even more dangerous. Once, over the high whine of the engine, he shouted, 'I think you're going to have to get out and push!' But Jo, although her head was painfully near the roof of the cab, was otherwise quite relaxed, for Adam handled the bucking vehicle with calm ease.

At last they rounded a low, rocky outcrop and Adam pulled up at the crest of a shallow valley. He pointed ahead of them. 'Qatrak.'

Jo, her eyes strained and gritty after hours of desert driving, stared at the expanse ahead then gradually she made out at the bottom of the valley, growing out of the sand as it seemed, a line of columns, golden in the late sun, and beyond them several clumps of palm trees and—marvellously—the soft glint of water. She was quite unable to speak and Adam let in the clutch and drove slowly down, to where the track petered out.

He leaned across and opened her door, saying, 'You go ahead—I'll sit here for a bit and recover.'

So Jo, her legs slightly unsteady—and not only from the journey—walked slowly over to the columns. Some were cracked and some lay broken on the ground, but they still managed to convey an impression of dignified serenity and pride. They ran alongside a paved road, its slabs worn by feet and wagons of several thousand years before and when the columns ended, the roadway went on for a few yards between ragged stone and clay brick walls, then disappeared into the sand.

Jo leaned against one of the walls, hot through her cotton clothes, and gazed around her, feeling the calm of the place take hold of her mind. The only noise was the soft rustle of the ribbed palm branches in the late afternoon wind which had sprung up—and the sound of Adam's door closing. She watched him come towards her and as he came close she stood up, feeling as though she were on tiptoe. Almost without realising it, she lifted her hands towards him, but at the sight of his face, closed and empty of expression they fell back by her side.

'Well, what do you think of it?'

She smiled up at him, her face radiant. 'It's—it's magic. The most beautiful place I've ever seen.'

'I thought you might be disappointed.' His eyes still wore that shuttered look, but nothing could damp her pleasure.

'Oh no—how could I be? All this——' She waved her arm in a wide sweep, taking in most of the Middle East, and he laughed.

'Well, make the most of it—it might just disappear.'

'Disappear? Like a mirage, you mean?'

'Not exactly, but the sand is greedy—like the sea. When I first came here there was much more to see, and the oasis was much bigger, but the sand's been burying them both for years.'

'But it mustn't be allowed to,' Jo exclaimed.

'I think it'll be all right. Now the petroleum industry's getting on its feet at last out here there's more money—and besides, they've asked UNESCO for help. A team of archaeologists are coming out to have a look soon, so don't worry too much.'

The wind stirred the palm leaves again as they walked back past the columns, their shadows slanting across the stones in the low sun. Back at the Land Rover, Adam began dragging out large bundles which Jo had hardly been aware of before.

'If you're not too hungry, we'll get the tents up before we eat. It's a job I don't like doing in the dark.'

Jo gaped at him. 'Tents?'

'Yes—oh, don't panic,' he added, with a sideways look at her, 'you've got one all to yourself.'

'No—I don't mean that. It's just that I——' Her voice trailed away and Adam, misunderstanding her silence, went on impatiently, 'I'm afraid four-star hotels are a bit thin on the ground round here, love. There's a caravanserai at the next oasis twenty miles on—but I've stayed in the odd one on occasion and, believe me, with bed bugs the size of beetles, and the sweet smell of old camel, you're better off out here, even if the company isn't all you might wish. And if you've got any ideas about moving on, forget them—I value my neck too much to try and drive back over that vile track in the dark. So come and help put the tents up.'

Jo, her mood deflated like a burst balloon, did as she was told and, after one mishap when she tripped over a guy rope and Adam snarled at her, the tents were up, between the Land Rover and the water's edge. She turned away towards the vehicle but Adam caught hold of her hand.

'Sorry, Jo—it's just that I'm a bit whacked. And it niggles me leaving a job half done, although I expect Ali will have got things moving again by now. All the same, I shouldn't have bitten your head off. You go and have a look round, while I fix us something to eat.'

She looked at him, seeing the strain in his face, and quite unexpectedly, found herself aching to hold him, to soothe away the lines of fatigue with her fingers. She caught herself up, horrified. 'No—*you* sit down, and I'll get some food sorted out,' and she turned towards the Land Rover, not wanting him to see her face.

As she dragged out the portable gas-stove and huge hamper of food that Stella had packed, he reached past her for a towel. 'I'm going to have a dip—I haven't got my trunks with me, I'm afraid, so avert your eyes to save your blushes.'

Jo chose not to reply but went on stolidly unpacking the food containers and when he came back, dressed and towelling his wet hair, she had piled plates with slices of tinned meat, salad and rolls, and was fighting away the flies. By the time they had eaten, the dusk had closed in silently all around them, and as they drank their coffee, which Adam brewed on the gas-stove, a huge yellow moon slid up through the trees at the far end of the oasis, touching everything with a faintly luminescent glow.

As she put down her empty coffee-cup, Jo thought dispassionately, this is a magical, marvellous moment, and, whatever else happens to me, I shall remember it all my life.

She glanced across at Adam, but he was leaning against the Land Rover, the dark bulk of his outline making a deeper shadow in the shade cast by the vehicle, and in a split second she felt the old feelings rise in her. She was afraid of this dark, silent shape, hunched into his own thoughts, as he cradled the coffee-cup in his hands. She sprang up and began abruptly bundling everything back into the hamper, glad to be doing something, making a noise.

Adam spoke from the shadow. 'Aren't *you* going to have a dip? You'd feel much better for it.'

'Oh—no, I'll just rinse my face and hands.'

'OK—just as you please.' He stood up and yawned, stretching himself. 'Well, if it's all right with you, I think I'll turn in. We'll make an early start tomorrow—our plane doesn't leave until mid-afternoon, but I'll allow time for a puncture, just in case. I've unrolled your sleeping-bag—

tuck yourself well in, the nights are cold.' Then, as she still stood by the vehicle, he added, 'Oh, and don't go getting any ideas about wandering off on your own, please. Goodnight, Jo—sleep tight.'

But that was just what she apparently was not going to do, Jo thought, two hours later, as she stared up at the roof of the tent, for although she was very tired sleep would not come. She had decided not to bother to change into her nightdress and had stayed in the loose cotton top and trousers and that had been a mistake, for although they had been comfortable enough all day, now every time she tossed back and forth they tied themselves in knots around her. And Adam had been right—she should have taken the chance for a bathe. She seemed to have sand all over her— under her nails, behind her ears, even her hair grated against the pillow, harsh with sand and sweat.

And besides, she felt very strange, almost heady, as though she were anticipating, waiting for something to happen which she didn't quite understand. It was no use— she would never get to sleep like this. She sat up and reached into her travelling bag for her nightdress and a towel, then crept out of the tent. The cold air struck her as she stood up and she hesitated, for the dark water of the pool now looked far less inviting, but then she remembered the scratchy sand against her sweat-sore skin.

The pool was only about forty yards long and Jo walked silently on tiptoe to the far end, terrified that she would disturb Adam. She stood still and listened, but there was no sound apart from a small eddy of wind rustling the dry branches of a clump of tamarisks, growing right on the water's edge. She pulled off her clothes and dropped them among the bushes then, not allowing herself time to think, she stepped into the pool.

Unlike the air, the water had retained some of the burning heat of the sun and its warmth was a pleasant surprise to her. The pool was shallow at the edge then, as she went deeper, she felt soft, oozing mud under her feet, so she struck out towards the centre, feeling the water close round her like smooth satin. She turned on her back and floated, running her fingers through her hair, fanning the strands out again and again, while above her the moon and a million stars hung in the sapphire sky. In this beautiful, timeless place, it was as if all the tensions, the sorrows and anxieties, not just of the past few days, but of the past years, were being washed away and she stretched her limbs lazily in the water, feeling rather like a chrysalis, splitting to reveal the new, untouched eager butterfly within.

'*Jo*! What the hell are you up to?'

She rolled over hastily, treading water, and through the darkness she could just make out the outline, a few yards away on the shore.

'Oh, I couldn't sleep for the sand all over me, so——'

'Well, you've got the sand off you now, so come on out.'

'Now, hang on, Adam. Just who do you think——'

'And just what do *you* think you're playing at, wandering off on your own? It's precisely what I told you not to do. So come on out, and get back to your tent.'

Something in his tone warned Jo that on this occasion it would be wiser not to argue any further—he was perfectly capable of diving in and dragging her out bodily. So, as he strode off in the direction of the tents, she waded to the shore in silence. He had spoiled everything for her and her joy had gone. She roughly towelled herself dry and pulled on her nightdress, her body glowing, then wrapped the towel turban-like round her hair.

As she came up to where he was standing he turned and she stopped, trying to force a light, careless laugh. 'Oh,

Adam, aren't you being just a little melodramatic?'

In two strides he had crossed the no-man's-land between them and had her by the shoulders, shaking her, his fingers digging into her flesh.

'Will you get it into your silly head?' The savagery in his voice startled her. 'The desert isn't your precious Compton Lydiatt! It can be a dangerous place, particularly at night. Not all the mountain lions are safely behind bars in Dhabra Zoo, you know!'

As she stared up at him, shocked, he released her abruptly. 'So don't you go off again—at least, not while I'm in charge of you. Now, for heaven's sake, Jo, get to bed.'

She stood quite still for a moment. 'I—I'm sorry, Adam. I suppose it *was* stupid of me.'

Her voice was small, almost timid. She hesitated, then when he did not reply she went to walk past him, desperate to reach the solitude of her tent. But he put out a hand to detain her.

'Oh, Jo.' It was all he said, but the naked longing in his voice stopped her dead.

His grip this time was gentle but the touch of his fingers made her quiver softly deep inside. He put his hand under her chin and tilted her face towards his. Both were a pale blur in the darkness but somehow he sensed her silent acquiescence, and with a jerky movement he gathered her to him. 'Oh, Jo, Jo, Jo.' He was murmuring her name over and over again as he rained a storm of kisses on her face, her hair, her throat. His voice clamoured in her ears, blotting out everything, so that she put her arms around him, and closed her eyes under his lips.

When he at last released her, she leaned against him for a few moments, breathless. Then, Adam gently held her away from him.

'Jo?' There was an unspoken question in his voice, and

she hesitated for a second.

'Jo, look at me.'

She raised her eyes to his, and through the pale glimmer of moonlight she saw his gaze—full of longing, desire, yes, but also a deep tenderness that made her heart leap. In that second's exchange of looks—more potent than a thousand words—she knew what it was she had been fighting against, not even once admitting it to herself, since his return—that under all the anger, resentment and fear she loved Adam, would always love him, and more than that— that there was no need any longer for fear. She knew instinctively that she was secure with him for ever, that he would never hurt her again.

She felt his grip slacken as he pulled the towel away so that her wet hair tumbled to her shoulders; his fingers, as they brushed her forehead, made her pulses race, and it was she who lifted her hand to caress his face. He seized her hand and smothered it with kisses, then drew her to him, so that she could feel the waves of heat from his body and his heart thudding under her cheek.

Silently, they sank together to their knees, seemingly in slow motion, as though the earth were giving way beneath them as they fell. The dark sand was clammy but Jo did not feel it. She was only aware of Adam's hand sliding under her nightdress, his fingers softly moving up over her thighs and stomach, leaving a trail of fire behind him, as he explored her body thoroughly, yet slowly, in total possession of himself.

His breath was faintly warm on her face and she heard his throat catch as his hand reached, then cupped her left breast, and she knew that he had felt her heart bounding against his sensitive fingers. He bent his head, and she felt his lips gently moving across her breast, encircling the nipple as in a ring of burning heat. Very deep inside her being, a slow fuse of fire was lit, and strange pinpricks fizzed within her like bursting bubbles of champagne. Just for one pulsebeat, a flicker of the old terror returned, but then an inexpressible rapture filled her whole mind and body and she thought, this is Adam and I love him. With a little sigh, she yielded herself to him, pulling him down to her, as her body arched to meet his.

Then, just as she waited for him to possess her completely, Adam went quite still in her arms. He rolled away from her and lay with his back to her, his breath rasping in his throat. After a few moments, he spoke, his voice so rough that she could hardly make out the words.

'Oh, Jo—I shouldn't have tried to—take advantage of you.'

'Take advantage of me—what do you mean?' Her voice trembled.

'Oh—getting you out here. The moon—the oasis— everything set for the soft seduction scene. But I'm not going to do that wrong to you again.' His voice was fierce. 'I'm not going to let myself!'

He rolled over and propped himself on one elbow looking down at her, his eyes shadowed. He took her hand. 'Marry me, Jo.'

'Yes—oh, yes, I'll marry you.'

Crushing her hand between his fingers until she almost cried out, he lifted it to his lips and kissed it. As their eyes met, she smiled at him, feeling light-headed, almost feverish with joy. She drew a deep, shuddering breath—after all the years of misery and heart-searching, it had finally been so easy, so very easy.

He sat up and gently kissed her forehead. 'You're cold. Stay here.' And he fetched a rug from the Land Rover, draping it round her and tucking it under her icy feet. Then he sat beside her again, his arm round her. The moon had emerged from behind a cloud and they could clearly see, on the far side of the oasis, the columns, etched against the hillside.

'I'm so glad you brought me here—it's——' she fumbled for the words '——it's so beautiful that it's as though we're in another world of our own.'

She sighed with contentment and leaned her head against him. He kissed her wet hair, then his lips moved round to her cheek and he trailed soft undemanding kisses down to her throat.

'Jo—I'm not going to lay a finger on you until we're married—so you'd better marry me tomorrow! I can't keep my hands off you much longer. I thought I loved you eight years ago, but now——' There was a catch in his voice and his arm tightened round her. 'When I think of all those wasted years.' His voice was desolate and she wanted desperately to lighten his mood.

'Oh, surely not completely wasted—I'm sure there's been a long procession of nubile young ladies.'

Adam turned her face to his. 'Listen to me, Jo. That first night I came to Pear Trees—I said then that over the past eight years *you'd* always got in the way. And it's the truth— oh, I tried to have relationships, to blot out the memory of you as much as anything, but you spoiled every other woman for me, and there was never a day—or a night— when I didn't ache for you. Now I'm going to marry you, and spend the rest of my life loving you.'

She took his hand, imprisoning it between her two smaller ones, stroking her thumb across his calloused palm. Slowly, dreamily, she said, 'And Jon and I—we'll move in with you . . . I can run Pear Trees just as well from the manor—it's only a few minutes if I cut through the hedge . . . And Bobbie can have Pigsties, if she wants to.'

The muscles in his arm stiffened, and she felt his whole body tense.

'It isn't quite as simple as that, I'm afraid, Jo.' His voice was very quiet, and a cold finger of unease slid down her spine. 'I'm bored out of my mind with business lunches, never-ending company meetings, endless travelling—the hotels may be palatial, but living out of a suitcase is—well, living out of a suitcase, whether it's Hong Kong, Caracas, or anywhere else.' She felt his eyes on her, in a searching gaze. 'Try to understand.' His voice was pleading.

'What are you trying to tell me, Adam?' Jo forced her voice to be cool, composed, although her throat was tight.

'This trip has decided me finally. The Rabbaq government—through Ali—has offered me a three-year contract to help develop the new petroleum field, and I intend to accept. I shall still remain as one of the consortium, but the others have agreed that I should concentrate on our petroleum interests. I shall probably come back to the UK when the work's finished, but for now—no.'

He looked at her questioningly but Jo was silent for a long time, then finally, she said huskily, 'It's all right, Adam.'

He gave a gasp of relief, drawing her to him. 'Oh, Jo— you won't regret it, I swear. You and Jon, you'll have a marvellous life out here. You've seen for yourself how——'

Jo put her hands on his chest and pushed him away from her. 'You didn't let me finish, Adam.' She paused, then spoke very rapidly. 'I was going to say that Jon and I will still live at Pear Trees, go on as before—we can join you for holidays and, after all, you'll get leave fairly often, won't you?'

She stopped suddenly and looked at him, but although they were near enough for her to feel his warm breath on her cheek, she could not see his expression or sense his mood.

'No, Jo.' There was an ache of sadness in his voice which almost brought tears to her eyes.

'What do you mean?'

'I mean, no, Jo. I haven't waited eight years, just to spend my life living apart from you.'

'But——'

'No buts, love. Think what an existence it would be—for us all.'

'But you don't understand.' There was real fear in her voice. 'I couldn't let Pear Trees go, just like that. I couldn't walk out on it all.' The ground beneath her was trembling. Adam was asking her for the impossible—to give up her beloved Pear Trees—to hand herself over completely to someone else, tied and bound. She tried to put her feelings into words he could understand. 'You see, Adam, it's just that for so long I've been the boss, in charge, running the restaurant, running my own life—and Jon's.'

'Yes, Jon.' Adam's voice was remote. 'Couldn't you consider giving it up, if not for yourself, for Jon?'

'Oh, yes, of course—for Jon.' She shuddered, conscious at last of the sand's damp chill, and stood up, hugging her arms to her. 'It's very neat, isn't it? I give up Pear Trees and all that I've worked for. And you—you get everything you want. Just answer me this, Adam—you knew about the job before we came out here, didn't you?'

'Yes—at least, it was more or less settled when I came out in the spring.'

She walked away and had reached her tent when Adam caught up with her and wrenched her round to face him. 'What's got into you?' His tone was harsh and peremptory.

'Just this, Adam Roker. I'm not giving up what I've worked for, for so long, for anyone—*anyone*—and I don't like anybody trying to set me up or manipulate my life for me. Don't protest your innocence—you knew about the job and you deliberately set out to trap me again—yes, again. It's a carbon copy of last time, isn't it? You thought if you spread the snare thickly enough with honey—your rich friends, luxury living—"all this can be yours, too, my dear"—I wouldn't be able to refuse.' Another horrible suspicion leapt into her mind. 'And Ali not coming back with us—just the two of us alone here—was that a put-up job between you to clinch the deal?' Adam gave a grunt of exasperation but she went on, 'And then you'd have got what you've really wanted all along.'

'And what's that?'

'Why, Jon, of course. He's what you're really after, isn't he?'

Adam muttered a furious exclamation. 'God, was there ever such a crazy, unreasonable female as you, Johanna? I just mentioned Jon's name and you fly straight off the handle. Shut up and listen to me,' he snapped as she began angrily to speak. 'OK, I admit I *did* try to show you the sort of life you—and *our* son—would have out here. I admit I did try to make you love me. Why do you think I moved into the Manor? Why did I take you to Hampstead, of all places? In fact, this whole business of the take-over seemed a heaven-sent opportunity to pick up your tracks again—although it was still quite a shock when you opened the door to me that first evening. And, yes, I admit that I made the most of Jon's illness. I did want to give him this holiday, of course—but it was *you* I was thinking of most. I thought if I got you away from Pear Trees, I might manage to make you see things a bit straighter. Surely that's no crime, even in *your* book? But you don't want to be my wife—or anyone else's, for that matter. What it comes down to is that you're—you're married to that damned restaurant of yours!'

He banged his fist into his palm with frustration. 'You told me when I first met you again that Pear Trees was enough for you—that it was your whole life. But I was fool enough to think if I loved you sufficiently, somehow I would make you love me.'

He took a deep breath, then continued, speaking slowly, deliberately, 'I want you most desperately, Jo—more than anything else I've ever wanted in my whole life.' His voice trembled and, against her will, she was moved by the empty sadness in it. 'But you're going to thwart me yet again—I know it.' He shook her angrily. 'I'm not prepared to share your affections. If you married me, you would *always* come first with me, and I would have to come first with you. I tell you this, Jo, I'm certainly not playing second fiddle to a—to a restaurant!'

He loosed his hold on her arms. 'I'm not arguing any more with you. It would be a waste of breath with someone as pigheaded as you. Now I'm going to try and get some sleep, and I advise you to do the same.' And he turned away to his tent.

'Oh, you—you——' Jo burst out, but he had gone, and all around her the desert was dark and empty.

CHAPTER THIRTEEN

'. . . Oh, and I'll just leave you these menus to look through, Jo. I'm off into Broadston now—we'll have a chat over coffee later this morning.' Bobbie's face was eager. 'We're all dying to hear about the trip.'

When she had gone, Jo began shuffling through the menu cards, but after a few minutes she laid them on the kitchen table and went to the window to stand staring out across the fields behind Pigsties. She felt a strange sense of unreality, almost of disorientation, which she supposed must be jet lag, as though part of her had not boarded the British Airways jet at Dhabra Airport the previous day.

The previous day! Jo almost shuddered at the memory. Any regrets she might have had over leaving had evaporated in the thin morning air of the desert—her one overwhelming desire had been to get *away*, to escape to the obscurity of Pear Trees. The journey back from the oasis was virtually silent—Adam had retreated into himself, leaving her far away, and she could only feel relief. She felt the same relief when, back at the bungalow, there was only time to finish packing, shower and have a quick lunch before leaving for the airport.

She decided to go upstairs. Their cases still lay sprawled over the bedroom floor, spilling their contents, and methodically she emptied Jon's case of all his dirty clothes, before starting on her own. As she did so, the memory of Stella's face as they had said goodbye rose before her—the questioning look in her eyes, the deep concern, which Jo had somehow managed not to see, as she had hugged her.

And Jasmin, helping her pack with tears in her eyes, for the girl had grown genuinely fond of Jon. Jo was glad now of the impulse which had made her tear the lovely silk dress, now mended, from its hanger and thrust it on her—after all, she would never wear it again. And the memory of Jasmin's astonished delight warmed her chill heart a little.

The long flight, with Jon sitting between them, and then the silent drive home, she would not allow herself to think of; but then, when she stood up with her arms full of clothes, she saw the white-wrapped box on her dressing-table. As Adam had lifted out their cases the previous night, he had fished it out of his pocket and pressed it on her, saying brusquely, 'I got it for you when I bought Carol's, so you might as well have it.'

She dropped the clothes on the bed and opened the box. Inside was a delicate pearly glass phial of perfume. Jo's heart twisted inside her, but she forced herself to go into the bathroom, open the medicine cabinet and push the bottle to the far corner of the bottom shelf. Then she scooped up the washing and went back downstairs, telling herself this first day was bound to be the worst.

The first day . . . the first week . . . the first month . . . She somehow got through the rest of the summer, the heaviness within her like a physical pain. She, who had always been so self-controlled, so disciplined, suffered the humiliation of sensing the staff almost tiptoeing around her in their anxious desire not to upset or annoy her in any way and, unreasonably, this only irritated her all the more. Her tan faded, the golden streaked hair became dull again, and her mind, too, became dull, so that when a letter arrived from the TV producer, regretting that budget restrictions would make it impossible to go ahead with the programme, she hardly bothered to read to the end, just passed it over to Bobbie without a word.

As for Mark, when he rang her, jubilantly, to announce that he had not only negotiated a highly satisfactory lease on her behalf but had also persuaded the syndicate to leave Pear Trees intact and minus Sir Giles' flights of fancy, she had wounded, even offended him by her patent lack of enthusiasm and gratitude.

September came, grey and drizzly, and Jon went back to school—gladly, for once, Jo thought, as she watched him run across the playground, guiltily relieved, no doubt, to be away from her withdrawn presence. By the time she got back, it was raining hard. She decided not to go over to the restaurant straight away as she usually did—she would have a quiet cup of coffee at Pigsties before starting the day's work. She had just sat down, when the internal phone rang. It was Phil, to ask her where she had put the grapes—he needed them for the Sole Véronique he was in the middle of making.

'Oh, Phil—I'm so sorry. I remember you asking me, but I completely forgot them. I'd better go into Broadston to get some.'

'Oh, not to worry, Jo. I'll use something else instead—I've a recipe for sole with prawns that I've been wanting to try. Oh—and Bobbie says to tell you that we're almost out of Sauternes—and we need a good Burgundy. Shall she see to it, or will you?'

'Tell her to carry on and organise it please, Phil—and I'm sorry about the grapes.'

Jo put down the phone and stared miserably out of the window. What was wrong with her? Her world was falling apart and she didn't seem able to stitch it up again. The routine of the restaurant, all the jobs—even the boring, everyday ones—that she had once revelled in, now seemed meaningless. 'You fool,' she told herself savagely, 'you fool. As if once wasn't enough for him to ruin your life, you've let him do it again, haven't you?'

She realised she was speaking aloud, the words reverberating through the quiet air, and she slammed her hands down hard on the kitchen table so that her cup and saucer bounced. 'Oh, damn you, Adam—I wish, how I wish, I'd never set eyes on you!'

She got to her feet and, holding her mac over her head, ran across to the restaurant. Work was her salvation, she thought, and for the next fortnight she worked in a self-absorbed intensity, not sparing herself or her staff in any way.

But then, one morning she woke, aching all over, her throat dry and tight. When she tried to sit up, she fell back on the pillow as the room spun round before her eyes. Jon got his own breakfast, and Bobbie took him off to school and rang the surgery, then Jo lay listlessly waiting for Doctor Grey's footsteps on the stairs.

He set down his bag unceremoniously. 'Now then, young lady, what's the matter with you?'

Jo struggled to sit up. 'I—I think I may have caught a bug, or something,' she faltered, and he listened while she explained about the holiday. Then he gave her a thorough going over and finally looked at her over the top of his glasses.

'Hmm, well—it's not 'flu, and I don't think you've picked up any fancy foreign bugs. Still, I'd better take a blood sample, just in case.' He carefully wrote out the label. 'What's today? Tuesday. Call in Friday lunchtime at the surgery—I should have the result by then. Oh, and stay in bed, if you don't feel any better—you look as though you could do with a rest.'

'But I've just had a rest,' Jo almost snarled at his retreating back, before throwing herself back on the pillows.

Daphne and the others refused to let her do anything except potter about and she was glad on Friday to drive up through the village to the surgery. Doctor Grey was there, packing drugs into his bag. 'Ah, Jo, come through.' She followed him into the consulting-room and sat down. 'I've had the results of your test. As I thought, quite clear, nothing wrong with you—physically.'

'But there must be. I could hardly get out of bed this morning.' Jo's eyes smarted with tears of self-pity.

'Are you perhaps still grieving for your aunt? You were very close—it would be quite natural——'

'For Aunt Joan? Oh, no, it's nothing to do with—at least, well, I suppose I am,' Jo concluded lamely, feeling she had betrayed herself. 'Look, could you prescribe a tonic—it's all I need.'

He looked across at her, frowning. 'Is he married? Is that what it is?'

'What do you mean?'

'Look, Johanna, I've known you since you were so high, ever since your aunt brought you to Lydiatt. So, as an old friend who's seen you through measles, mumps and everything else, let me speak plainly. There's nothing wrong with you physically, you haven't got any exotic bugs, you assure me you aren't grieving for your aunt, I know that restuarant of yours is doing well—so, QED, it's a man. Is he married?'

Jo was past protesting. 'No—no,' she stammered.

'Well, this is my prescription, young lady—marry him, or forget him, one or the other. And now—I've got calls to make.'

Marry him, or forget him—the words came in the rhythm of the car wheels as she drove back. Well, she had got over Adam once, and she would do it again—and for the next week she threw herself even more strenuously into her work, hoping that this was the best way to conquer her weakness.

It was the following Friday that Bobbie asked tentatively, 'How are you feeling now, Jo?'

'Oh, much better, thanks. I expect it was the strain of getting ready to go on the trip in such a rush—and the heat was a bit much.'

'Well, if you feel well enough, I'd like next weekend off.'

Jo stared at her. 'Next weekend off?'

'Yes—and Phil. He—wants to come up to Newcastle to meet my family.' Bobbie was blushing as Jo gaped at her across the table.

'But—but it's impossible, Bobbie. I couldn't possibly manage with both of you off.'

The girl's smile clouded but she nodded slowly. 'Yes, I suppose it would be a bit difficult, Jo. Don't think any more about it—we can go another time, perhaps.'

She picked up the walnut coffee gâteau she had been icing and went through with it into the cold room, leaving Jo standing at the kitchen table, toying with a piping-bag. How could she have missed this romance that had obviously been flowering right under her nose? Had she become *so* self-centred? For heaven's sake, she told herself fiercely, how could you be so selfish, so niggardly, after all that girl's done for you?

She followed her into the cold room. 'Bobbie, I'm sorry—of course you can go. We'll cope all right.'

'But are you sure——'

'Sure? Of course I'm sure.' Jo forced a bright smile.

'Well, we *could* leave early on Sunday morning.'

'No you won't, you'll leave first thing Saturday morning—and that's an order. You deserve a break, both of you.'

And it seemed to Jo, after breakfast on the Monday, that

the hard work of the weekend had done her good, for she felt livelier than she had done for weeks. That evening she was on her own, for Jon was at a birthday party, when they arrived back, Bobbie bursting in radiant-eyed to show her the sparkling ring on her finger.

Jo kissed her. 'Dear Bobbie, I'm sure you'll both be so very happy—but I hope you're not planning to leave me next week, or anything——'

But Bobbie was not listening to her. She was delving in her bag and chattering excitedly. '. . . and Jo, remember how we talked ages ago—oh, it was after that journalist came—about doing weekend teas—you know, log fire and so on—well, I was telling my Gran about it and she said her mother used to be cook at a big house in North Yorkshire, and——' she brought out a sheaf of tattered papers and laid them on the table with an air of triumph '——Gran found her old recipes and she's lent them to me. There's a list somewhere of the things she said were cooked when Edward the Seventh came to tea—lemon whisky cake, singing hinny, ginger parkin . . .'

By the time Bobbie had gone, clutching her precious recipes, Jo's head was almost splitting with the effort of trying to appear as pleased and excited as she knew she ought, and she decided she would have to take a couple of paracetamol tablets. But the dragging pain in her head and neck made her clumsy and as she took out the tablets from the medicine cabinet her hand brushed against another bottle and it crashed down against the edge of the bath, shattering on the floor at her feet.

Dully, she stared down at the fragments of glass then, realising what it was, she caught her breath in a half-sob and knelt down. There was one piece of the pearly glass bottle intact, and she picked it up and cradled it in her hands. As she did so, she inhaled the warm musky fragrance which drifted up to her and wrapped itself round her, bringing with it the memories she had tried to push away forever.

For a long time she knelt on the floor, leaning against the washbasin, her head on her hand, staring unseeing at the broken bottle. It was as though the perfume was the one missing piece of a jigsaw which she had begun in Rabbaq—or even before—and had been completing here: her behaviour of the last weeks, her careless acceptance of the new lease, her reaction to Bobbie's plans. Now this final piece slotted into place and she was forced to see what she had refused absolutely to see for weeks.

She cared nothing for Pear Trees. She wasn't interested any longer in her once beloved restaurant—log fires ... parkin ... candlelit teas ... She couldn't care less. There was only one thing she wanted, and she had thrown it away wilfully, deliberately, childishly—and for the *second* time. It was not Adam, but she herself who had enacted a carbon copy scene—*she* was the one who had been prepared to sacrifice her happiness—and Jon's—for a mere *thing*, just as she had refused Adam eight years previously.

Slowly, Jo stood up, feeling stiff and cold. One thought hammered at her brain, over and over. Was it too late? Or could she this time break the mould? On an impulse, she swung round, her feet crunching the tiny glittering shards of glass, and ran headlong downstairs.

She snatched down an old plastic mac of Aunt Joan's, the nearest thing to hand, and ran across the courtyard and through the garden in the pouring rain. Only when her feet squelched under her did she remember that she had on thin canvas espadrilles. Once over the stream, she pushed through the dripping rhododendrons and out on to the wide lawns of the Manor. In the dusk, she could just make out the scaffolding ranged across the south front of the old house.

She knew that Adam's flat and the company office were in the wing by the stables so she went in that direction. But then she stopped as she registered that there were no lights on in the house, not a single one. Adam was not there—for that matter, he might not have been there for weeks. None of her staff would have dared to mention his name, much less announce that he had departed for good. Adam! As she allowed herself to remember his face, his body, his hands caressing her, a searing pain flooded through her. She had shut the memories out for so long and, now that it was too late, an aching desire to be near him took possession of her.

She tried the office door; to her surprise, it opened. But now it was almost dark and she could only see that the room was empty. At the far side of the room was a flight of stairs which she guessed must lead up to his flat. He wasn't there but that was the only place now where she could feel herself near to him, so she went up them. On the landing she paused, then, hardly knowing what she was doing, turned the handle; it opened under her hand and she walked in.

To her amazement, the room was faintly illuminated by several candles, roughly stuck on to saucers in a row on the table, on which were also the remains of a meal. From an open door beyond she saw the pale glow of more candles and when she looked inside she saw that it was a bedroom. Then, as she stood irresolute, she heard footsteps running up the stairs outside and she turned back into the sitting-room just as Adam came in. He was right in the room before he saw her, then he stopped dead.

'Jo?'

A nervous laugh bubbled up past her lips. 'Oh, I was just thinking this must be a new *Marie Celeste*,' she burst out, and when he stared at her, his dark eyes gleaming in the candlelight, she giggled again, then babbled on, 'You know—the meal on the table, the candles burning, but all the crew gone, or something like that. Of course, you could be a ghost, I suppose. You're not, are you?' She put her hand up to her head. 'Oh, Adam, there's something I wanted to tell you—only I do feel very peculiar . . .'

When she came to, she was lying on his bed and he was bending over her. He hoisted her up and pushed a glass between her lips. 'Drink this.'

'What is it?'

'Just a drop of whisky in hot water and lemon—it may possibly stop you getting pneumonia.'

She sipped it, then, as she handed him the glass, realised that someone had made a very thorough job of undressing her and putting her into a thick dressing-gown; she even had socks on.

'Sorry about that,' he said, 'but you were boiling hot and drenched right through. Whatever have you been doing—twenty lengths of the lake?'

She did not seem able to reply directly. 'What are the candles for? Is there a power-cut?'

He laughed mirthlessly. 'There is here. The electricians have been down in the cellar trying to fix up some subdued spotlighting for Giles's wretched waxworks, and they managed to fuse the entire system. In the end, I told them to leave it till tomorrow. Look—if you feel all right, let's go into the other room, by the gas fire—it's chilly in here for you.'

Before she could move, he had caught her up into his arms and carried her through into the sitting-room. He did not put her down though, just stood holding her, their eyes level. She began nervously fidgeting with his tie, feeling she must speak but finding it very difficult.

'Adam——' she began, and stopped.

'Jo?' His face was serious and the expression in his eyes made her stomach turn over.

'Adam, I'm—that is—oh, Adam, I've been so miserable.'

The corners of her mouth turned down and she laid her head against his shirt and began to sob, loud, tearing sobs that racked her whole body. Adam sat down on the sofa, still cradling her in his arms, hushing her as though she were a baby, stroking her wet hair, until at last the sobs subsided, apart from an occasional quiver. He handed her a large white handkerchief and she mopped her eyes then sat up, pushing the wet strands of hair off her face and giving him a shy smile.

'Thank goodness for candlelight. What a *mess* I must be.'

'Jo-Jo,' he said softly, and gave her a look that made her heart turn half a dozen somersaults, then he put up his hand and caressed her cheek. 'My golden girl.'

Jo wrinkled up her nose. 'Not that much of a girl. I'm nearly—oh, good grief, I'd completely forgotten. It's my birthday on Friday!'

He lifted her off his lap. 'Well, in that case, you'd better have this—just a few days in advance.' He went to a drawer and took out a small package. 'Close your eyes and hold out your hands.' Wonderingly, she obeyed and held out her cupped hands. 'Now open them.'

The necklace was even more lovely than she remembered, the smooth polished amber glowing translucent through the fretwork of gold threads and she gazed at him, speechless, across the beautiful thing.

When she at last found her voice, she stammered, 'But—but when did you get it?'

He laughed. 'Oh—just a bit of nifty footwork while you and Ali were talking by the Land Rover.' He got up. 'I'll just give Bobbie a ring at Pear Trees—I think she was afraid you might have thrown yourself into the lake, or something.'

He disappeared into the bedroom and she heard him talking and laughing. When he returned a few minutes later, she was struggling with the clasp of the necklace. He knelt in front of her and, brushing her hair out of the way, screwed up the intricate gold clasp. She looked down at the necklace.

'Thank you, Adam. It's—it's the most lovely thing I've ever had.' Her voice trembled slightly.

He affected to study it critically, then said, 'Still, my old dressing-gown doesn't exactly do much for it. Sit still a moment.'

Very slowly, he drew down the loose neck of the gown, leaving her shoulders and the top of her breasts exposed, so that the necklace fell gleaming against her bare skin. Jo thought he would kiss her then but, still kneeling in front of her, he only very softly brushed his hand down over her throat and the line of her shoulder. His eyes were intent on hers and she realised suddenly the unspoken question in them.

Her answer, too, was unspoken. She slid off the sofa, on to her knees, and began, very deliberately, one by one undoing the buttons on his shirt. As he had done to her, she pulled the shirt down from his shoulders, then laid her face against his chest and began dropping soft kisses on his skin, feeling his pulses quicken and throb under her. Then, as there was no other reaction from him, she took some of the soft dark hair between her teeth and teased at it, gently at first, then harder, until he gave an exclamation of pain.

'Ow—that hurt, you little savage. I'll make you suffer for that!' But then his face changed and he said quickly, 'I didn't mean that, my darling.'

Jo looked up at him, her eyes brimming with mischief.

'Oh dear—what a pity!'

His laugh was without constraint and he put his arm round her, but she suddenly remembered something he had said and jerked upright.

'Did you say you'd been round to *Pear Trees*? Surely not to see me?'

Not looking at her, he replied slowly, 'Yes, I did actually. There was something I wanted to tell you.' He stopped, as if waiting for her to speak, but when she stayed silent he went on, 'I went to tell you that I've decided to stay here—I'm not going back to Rabbaq.'

'But what about your work? You wanted to go back so much. Why?'

'Can't you guess?'

The candlelight was full on his face and Jo saw for the first time the lines of strain around his mouth, the crease between his eyes, and her heart smote her. All these weeks, she had been so engrossed in her own private world of desolation that she had never spared Adam's feelings one single thought, but now she saw that he had been suffering at least as badly as she herself had.

Thrusting down all her innate reserve, she took his hand and said, 'Adam, listen to me. I know I've been a fool, a stupid blind fool, but not any longer. Pear Trees means nothing, nothing at all to me, I realise that now—I don't care if it falls down. And I'm not going to lose you for a second time for it—I love you too much. You're going back to Rabbaq, and Jon and I are coming with you—that is,' she hesitated, then said softly, 'if you still l-love me.'

He didn't look at her and said nothing, until at last she went on, unable to bear the silence any longer, 'Of course, I'd have to be sure there would be a good school for Jon—he's getting on so well here.'

'Oh, yes,' he said slowly, 'Ranji and his brother go to an

excellent preparatory school. There'd be no problem there.'

Then, at long last, he turned to look at her. 'Oh, Jo,' he said, his voice breaking, and at the transparent love and longing in his eyes, she almost broke down herself and cried again. She gathered him to her, holding his head to her breast, stroking and kissing his dark hair.

A long time later, they were sitting side by side on the sofa. Adam gently kissed her cheek. 'Don't look so sad, love. What is it?'

She smiled at him. 'Oh, nothing—it's just that I can't help regretting how much we've missed over the last eight wasted years.'

But he said quickly, 'Don't think about them, don't think about the past. Remember what you told me once—you can't bring back yesterday. Well—if we spend all our time pining for the past, we won't be able to get on with tomorrow. And we'll have some wonderful tomorrows, I promise you.'

'Yes, you're right.' She smiled happily at him.

'But what do you intend to do about Pear Trees?'

'Oh, I don't know—let Sir Giles turn it into a take-away.'

But he shook his head, looking serious. 'Look, Jo, I don't want to take it away from you completely—you've put far too much of yourself into it for that.' A thought struck him. 'I tell you what—let's see if Bobbie would like to take over as manager—she deserves the chance, doesn't she? And you can still keep your financial interest in it, of course—after all, I've always fancied marrying a rich woman!'

'Hmm, and I rather fancy the role of *sleeping* partner!' Her eyes sparkled wickedly, but then she added, 'Mind you, Adam, I shan't want to spend three years in Rabbaq, just lounging by a swimming-pool—I'd go mad with boredom.'

'I'm sure you would—and Stella doesn't either, you know. She's set up a girls' club in downtown Dhabra, and she also helps at the new city hospital. You could work with her, or find something of your own to do. Oh, and talking of hospitals,' the devilment was back in his eyes, 'the maternity services in Dhabra are particularly good, I believe, as Stella can vouch for!'

She pulled a face at him. 'Hey, let's get married, shall we, before you start planning my future career in quite so much detail?'

'My thoughts exactly—and that's why you'd better get dressed. Your clothes should be dry now—I've had them by the fire in the bedroom.'

She looked at her watch. 'I must go soon, anyway. Jon's at a birthday party—they've gone swimming and I have to fetch him by nine.'

He stood up and pulled her to her feet. 'Fine. Let's go and fetch him—together.' Then, as she was disappearing into the bedroom, he called after her, 'I really do think, all things considered, that it's about time I made an honest woman of you, don't you?'

When she came back, Adam was standing in the middle of the room, in his overcoat. Just for a moment, their eyes met in a look of shared contentment, then he held out his arms and she went into them.

The rain had just about stopped and she walked serenely out to the car. Adam was right. Yesterday was finished—but tomorrow, oh, tomorrow would be marvellous—for the rest of their lives.

WINNING TALENT

Mills & Boon are proud to present their
1987 New Author Selection.
Four recently discovered exciting authors with a unique talent for
creating the very best romantic fiction. Love, drama and passion.
From the best of Mills & Boon's newcomers.

1. **Jeanne Allan** – **The Waiting Heart**
2. **Elizabeth Power** – **Rude Awakening**
3. **Katherine Arthur** – **Cinderella Wife**
4. **Amanda Browning** – **Perfect Strangers**

Price: £4.80   Mills & Boon   Available:
August 1987

Available from Boots, Martins, John Menzies, W.H. Smith,
Woolworths and other paperback stockists.

❀ ROMANCE

Next month's romances from Mills & Boon

Each month, you can choose from a world of variety in romance with Mills & Boon. These are the new titles to look out for next month.

NO ESCAPE Daphne Clair
TOUCH ME IN THE MORNING Catherine George
SUBSTITUTE LOVER Penny Jordan
THE WILDER SHORES OF LOVE Madeleine Ker
ECHO OF PASSION Charlotte Lamb
AN IMPOSSIBLE MAN TO LOVE Roberta Leigh
THE DOUBTFUL MARRIAGE Betty Neels
ENTRANCE TO EDEN Sue Peters
WHERE EAGLES SOAR Emily Spenser
PURE TEMPTATION Sara Wood
*****RELUCTANT WIFE** Lindsay Armstrong
*****MAN SHY** Valerie Parv
*****SHADOWS** Vanessa Grant
*****HUSBAND REQUIRED** Debbie Macomber

Buy them from your usual paperback stockist, or write to: Mills & Boon Reader Service, P.O. Box 236, Thornton Rd, Croydon, Surrey CR9 3RU, England. Readers in Southern Africa — write to: Independent Book Services Pty, Postbag X3010, Randburg, 2125, S. Africa.

*These four titles are available from Mills & Boon Reader Service.

Mills & Boon
the rose of romance

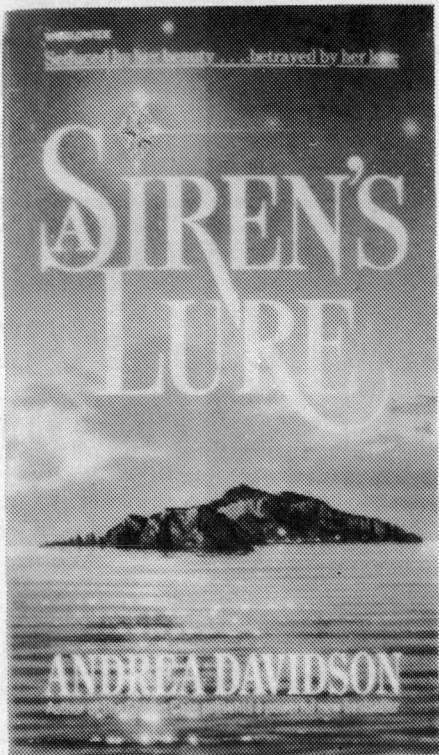